THE TRAVELERS

DETECTIVE CLUB

AN ORIGIN STORY

SUSSI VOAK

Also by Sussi Voak

The Travelers Detective Club Portugal

The Travelers Detective Club Paris

The Travelers Detective Club San Francisco Bay Area

Interested in a story about how Devon, a detective in books one through three, becomes a member of the club? Join Sussi's newsletter by going to her website at sussivoak.com and a free story will arrive in your inbox. (Or your parents' inbox!)

i

ISBN -13 978-1-7340093-6-1

Cover illustration by Dede Nugraha

Chapter heading design by Zievonya on Fiverr

DEDICATION

To all the children who have had to grow up during the COVID-19 pandemic. You are resilient. Now go out and make some magic of your own.

Table of Contents

The Travelers Detective Club

Detective Club

An Origin Story

Chapter 1

Ten-year-old Travis hung his head as he walked home from school. Nothing was going right. He'd received a low mark on his math homework, gotten in trouble for talking in class even though the room at the time was noisy and full of everyone's chatter, and the school bully stole his lunch money, again. Hungry, sad, and feeling incredibly alone, he trudged down the sidewalk. He hated everything about school; the disgusting bathrooms, his fifth-grade teacher, homework. He kicked at a rock and missed. Typical.

His mom wouldn't be home for an hour. At the start of the school year, she'd been nervous about leaving him home alone, but she had to work, and he'd convinced her he'd be okay, and he was. Except today. Today, he would have liked to be greeted at the door with a hug and some homemade chocolate chip cookies.

A medium-sized box set off to the side of the porch caught his eye as he unlocked the door. He did a double take. Sprawled in large block letters across the brown paper wrapping was his name. The package didn't have a return address. In his hand it weighed next to nothing, which surprised him.

Curious, he tore open the box as he stepped into the house. Inside lay a stuffed toy eagle. Light-blue wings overlaid an orange body, yellow eyes matched its legs. The colors made for a very odd-looking bird. Travis held the eagle up to his face. It blinked.

"AHHHH!" He screamed, dropped it, and ran into the kitchen.

No sound came from the living room. He peered around the corner. He didn't see anything. There was nothing on the floor except the empty box. He tiptoed across the carpet, simultaneously wanting to find the bird and run from the house. The eagle stood upright on the couch, ten feet from where Travis had dropped it. Travis stood frozen, staring at the eagle's back, unsure what to do.

A minute went by, then two. He stared at the eagle, waiting for he wasn't sure what, but nothing happened. Travis's stomach growled. Having missed lunch, he needed some food. With difficulty, he made his legs move and walked into the kitchen. He glanced over his shoulder before opening the fridge. Nothing.

While taking the raspberry jam out of the refrigerator, he thought he heard something and spun around. Still nothing. He pulled the peanut butter out and spread a generous amount on a slice of Wonder Bread. He loved Wonder Bread. The combination of sticky peanut butter and the white bread that on its own could stick to the top of his mouth had to be his favorite thing in the world. Sure enough, his mouth glued shut on the first bite. After grabbing milk from the fridge, he turned to get a glass and froze midstep. He would have screamed, but again, he couldn't open his mouth.

The eagle perched on the kitchen counter. It ruffled its feathers. The half-gallon container of milk slipped out of Travis's hand and onto the floor. He squatted down and reached for the milk, not taking his eyes off the bird. After missing it twice, his hand found the carton that, miraculously, was still upright.

"Hello. I am Baako." The dignified voice demanded attention. It paused, as if awaiting a response. Travis's eyes widened. He tried to swallow but couldn't. He needed to unglue his mouth.

The two stared at one another. Travis's eyes watered, determined as he was not to blink. Desperate for something to drink, he took a swig from the carton. His mom would kill him if she were home. Needing to tilt his head back, he broke eye contact. Finally able to swallow, the tension in his body eased, though only slightly. "Who are you?"

"I am Baako."

"No, no I got that. But who are you? Or, what are you?"

"Is that not clear? I am an eagle."

"Yeah, no offense, but you're a … you look like a stuffed animal with really weird coloring."

"Be that as it may, we have more important things to discuss."

Travis took another bite of his sandwich, followed closely by a gulp of milk. He kept his gaze on the bird. "How are you talking? You got batteries or something?"

"What are batteries?"

"They're these things you put in toys to make them work."

"I am not a toy," the stuffed bird said.

"You look like a toy."

"Well, I assure you I am not."

"Prove it."

"Excuse me?" Baako's eloquent voice filled the room.

"Prove it." He took another bite of his sandwich. "Pwoof youf want a troy."

The bird cocked its head.

Travis held up his index finger. He took a drink of milk and swallowed. Twice. "Prove you're not a toy."

Baako seemed to consider the request. Without warning, she flew at Travis, who threw his arms up in front of his face. The bird swiped what was left of his sandwich out of his hand.

"Hey!"

Back on the kitchen counter, the eagle tilted its head back to swallow the sandwich.

"I wouldn't do that," Travis said. "At least not all in one—"

But the sandwich disappeared, the only evidence, a bulge protruding from the eagle's neck. Its eyes grew wide.

"I told you." Travis grabbed a small bowl, filled it with water, and put it down in front of the bird.

"What's that for?" Baako asked.

"For the … you got it down? You're right. You are magical."

A car pulled into the driveway. "Oh, that's Mom. You can't be here." He grabbed the bird, picked up the box he'd dropped in the entryway, and ran down the hall to his room.

***

"Travis? I'm home." His mom's voice reached him as he shoved the eagle under his bed.

"Stay there," Travis insisted.

"Why is there milk all over the floor?" his mom called out as he came into the room.

"Hi, Mom. Umm, sorry. I thought I cleaned it up."

"You call this cleaned up?"

A puddle of milk the size of a small plate dirtied the floor. "Sorry." He grabbed a handful of paper towels and wiped up the mess.

"How was your day?" his mom asked as he discarded the soaked towels in the garbage.

The question caught him off guard, though she asked it every day. He'd forgotten about his awful school day after meeting Baako. As he turned to face her, his shoulders slumped.

"That good, eh?"

He nodded.

She wrapped him in a hug. "You hungry?"

"Yeah." He stepped back as his mom let go. "Roger stole my lunch money again." Travis grimaced. Oops. He hadn't meant to say that. He'd never told his mom about the school bully.

His mom, with one hand on the refrigerator door, spun around. "What do you mean, Roger stole your lunch money, *again*? Who's Roger?"

Travis took a deep breath and let it out. He hung his head.

"Don't you put your head down like that. Hold yourself high. You are one amazing human!"

"Yes, Mama." It came out in a whisper.

"What?"

He stood tall and met his mother's gaze. "Yes, Mama."

She stood waiting.

"I am one amazing human."

"There you go. Now sit down, and tell me what's going on while I make you a quesadilla."

So he told her about the bully, about the low grade on his math homework, and about getting into trouble in class.

"Why were you talking in class?" She slid the quesadilla onto a plate and placed it on the counter.

He shrugged and took a bite of his snack.

"Don't you shrug at me. Why were you talking in class?"

"We'd all just come in from recess. Everyone was talking."

His mom raised her left eyebrow.

"I swear!"

"Do I care about what everyone else was doing?"

Travis hung his head. Could this day get any worse? "The teacher just walked in and picked me out," he mumbled.

"What you mean? Picked you out?"

"Mom, half my friends weren't even sitting down. He hadn't started class yet. But he yelled at me to be quiet." A single tear, caused by the injustice he felt, fell down his cheek.

"Is that what happened?"

He nodded.

"Well then, we can just forget about it."

"You're not mad?"

"At you?" Mama said. "Not at all. But you need to mind yourself, even more than the other kids. Even—" she raised her voice as he was about to protest—"if it doesn't seem fair." She gazed intently into his eyes. "You got it?"

"Yeah," he said dejectedly.

"How about," his mom grabbed something out of the cupboard, "we open this?" She pulled out a Sara Lee coffee cake.

Travis smiled. "Yes!"

Chapter 2

Back in his room, Travis found the stuffed eagle perched on top of his bed, next to his pillow.

"You didn't really expect me to stay under that bed? Although I did find an interesting book."

"Hey, I've been looking for that."

"So," Baako said as Travis picked up the book and dusted it off, "are you at all curious why I'm here?"

Travis flung the paperback onto his bed and fell into a beanbag in the corner of his room. "Sure."

"Once upon a time there was an evil wizard—"

"Seriously? You're not making this up?"

Baako stared at him.

"Sorry, go on." He leaned back into the beanbag.

"Once upon a time there was an evil witch—"

"Wait a second," Travis interrupted. "A second ago you said there was an evil wizard, and now you're saying there's an evil witch." He sat up out of his beanbag. "You *are* making this up."

"Yes, yes, I'm sorry." Baako preened under her right wing, dislodging a thread. "I found myself in a box. The one you opened up, actually. I don't remember anything except—" Baako paused, her attention drawn to the piece of thread next to her on the bed.

Travis followed her gaze. The thread glowed. It unraveled, or was it multiplying?

"Um, what's happening?"

Baako didn't answer, her eyes trained on the bed cover where the single strand had grown into a ball of thread. No, fur. No. Before Travis could figure it out, a light emanated from its center, building and growing. A flash of light caused him to turn away. When he turned back, a stuffed orange cat with a white head and miniature black lines over its body sat on the bed.

"Interesting," Baako said. She proceeded to pull three more threads from under her wing before Travis spoke up.

"Stop! Just stop!"

"Don't you find this interesting?"

"I … I …" Travis couldn't find his words. He stared at the bed as light grew from the three masses and seemed to explode. In addition to the cat, an opossum, duck, and owl now rested on his comforter. The cat licked its back, the owl flapped its wings, the duck waddled up to Travis's pillow, stood on one leg and put its head under its wing. The opossum rolled over and played dead.

"Dear me, you do seem overwhelmed." Suddenly, the animals stopped moving, appearing to be simple stuffed animals. "There," Baako said, "is that better?"

"Yes…. No…. I don't know." Travis rubbed his hands over his tight black curls. "What am I supposed to do with you?" His gaze turned to the now motionless animals on the bed. "With them?"

"Oh, yes, I never finished my story." Baako started to groom herself and then stopped, possibly thinking better of it. "What I started to say was that I don't remember much of anything before finding myself in the box, except that whomever put me there was in a panic. The person said something about an evil …" Baako paused. "A warlock. That's what it was. Not a witch or wizard, a warlock."

"What's a warlock?" Travis asked.

"No idea. A witch or a wizard, I suppose."

Travis cocked his head, scrunching his forehead.

"I was to find a person, preferably a child, and they would help me. Then he threw me into that box." The eagle turned its head and eyed the box as if it were an evil being.

"What do you need help with?" Travis asked. He studied the creatures on his bed, expecting them to move again.

"With fighting an evil warlock, of course."

"Of course." Travis got up from his beanbag and paced his room. "The only problem is, I'm a ten-year-old kid who doesn't believe in magic."

"Even now?"

"Well …" he paused, deciding to ignore the question. "And even if there was a magic warlock or magician or whatever, why is that my problem? And what am I supposed to do about it?"

"My guess is that the warlock will have followed me here or will find me soon, which makes it your problem."

"You … you led him here?" Travis clasped his hands on top of his head. "Why … why would you do that?"

"I did not do so intentionally." Baako ruffled her feathers. "And as I said, it is my guess, and only my guess."

"Travis," his mom called out. "Dinner."

"Coming," he yelled back. Still eyeing the bird, he said, "I've got to go. I'll be back after dinner."

***

"Whoa. Hey, sport, slow down." Travis's dad watched him curiously. "What's your rush?"

Travis paused, his fork of mashed potatoes halfway to his mouth. "Just hungry," he lied.

His dad's eyebrows rose.

"Maybe," his mom said, "you're hoping you can get out of telling your father what happened at school today."

Travis lowered his fork. "I thought we were done with that? We already talked about it."

"Yes, but I think your father would like to know."

Travis sighed before telling his dad about his teacher and getting bullied at school. He was pretty sure his parents had already talked. They usually did. And, while his mother had narrowed in on the trouble with his teacher, his dad addressed his Roger problem.

"Is he one of the older kids?"

Nodding, Travis swallowed his potatoes. "Fifth grader like me. But huge."

"Are you the only one he bullies?"

Travis shook his head.

"Have you told your teacher or another adult?"

"Are you crazy? I'll get beaten up after school, or laughed at."

"What makes you say that?" his dad asked.

"'Cause that's what Roger said."

"Well, Roger most likely said that so you wouldn't tell on him."

"Dad!" he protested. "I can't tell on him."

"Travis. If you see someone starting a fire … Scratch that. If you saw a fire, a small fire, in a building, what would you do?"

"Call the fire department," Travis answered, confused by the question.

"Why?" his dad asked.

"So the fire wouldn't spread and burn the house down."

"Exactly."

He eyed his dad. "I don't get it."

"Bullies like Roger grow like wildfires. If no one calls them out, reports or stands up to them, they get bigger."

His dad pointed his fork at him. "It's a smart survival strategy, not confronting someone much bigger than you. But it allows the fire to spread. The bully terrorizes more and more of the school."

"That sounds like Roger."

"So when the fire gets really big, what happens? Can one firefighter put it out?"

"No. They have to call all the fire trucks."

"So find the other fire trucks at your school."

"Huh?" Travis scrunched his eyes.

"Find the other kids who have been bullied. Go together and talk to the principal or a teacher. There's strength in numbers, sport."

Travis smiled. He caught his mom smiling at his dad over the rim of her water glass.

***

Up in his room after dinner, Travis tried to engage Baako, but she was asleep, or completely ignoring him.

***

The next day was Friday and on impulse, Travis stuffed the opossum, duck, owl, and cat into his backpack.

"What?"

"Hey?"

"Um?"

"Excuse me?"

Each of the animals protested as Travis put them in.

"What do you think you're doing?" Baako said from the highest shelf in the room. Only she had had enough sense to move out of reach.

"I'm taking you with me."

"Why?"

"Because my friend Marcus might know what to do."

"He might know what to do about what?" Baako pressed.

"About you ... them." Travis eyed his backpack. "About all of this." He returned his gaze to Baako. "I need to get to school. Are you coming?"

"I think not."

Baako and Travis stared at each other. Travis broke contact first, said, "Fine," and zipped his bag closed.

Chapter 3

Eastside Elementary School was only five blocks away, so Travis walked to school. Those five blocks could be fast and easy or long and tortuous. It all depended on who he met along the way. He zipped up his sweatshirt against the chill of the morning; spring supposedly started last week, but someone forgot to tell whomever was in charge of the weather. Travis hugged his dad goodbye—his mom had already left for work—and headed out the door.

Three blocks away from home but two long blocks from school, Travis approached the end of a building just as Roger rounded the corner. The two walked right into each other. Travis's head hit Roger's chest.

"What'd you do that for?" Roger pushed him away.

While Travis's instinct was to lower his head and apologize, the words his mom made him repeat the night before insisted he not. "I am one amazing human," he muttered under his breath.

"What'd you say?" Roger took a step toward him.

Travis stood his ground. "I didn't say anything to you. And I didn't do anything to you. We walked into each other. It's no big deal."

He tried to walk away, but Roger stepped to the side, blocking him. Now Travis may have told his parents that Roger was a really big fifth grader, and while that may have been true, it wasn't the whole truth. Roger didn't start kindergarten until almost seven and repeated second grade. While Travis was ten, Roger was twelve. Also, his parents were probably giants. He was that big.

Travis took a step to the left. Roger matched him. Travis tried again, only to be blocked again.

"Come on, man!" Travis complained. Roger grabbed his backpack and pulled it off his body.

"Let's see what you have in here."

"Don't." He reached for his bag, but Roger held it away from him, unzipped it, turned it upside down and dumped its contents. Out poured four stuffed animals, a water bottle and a sack lunch.

Roger bent over, laughing. "You're kidding me. You have a bag full of stuffed animals?"

Travis's cheeks flushed. He bent down to pick up his belongings. Roger grabbed his lunch.

"Hey, that's mine!"

"Not anymore," Roger said. He picked up the stuffed cat off the ground before Travis had a chance to and held it up to his face. "Aw, the twirp likes his little stuffies."

Suddenly, the cat hissed, extended his claws, and slashed at Roger's face.

"AAAHHHHH!" Roger dropped the cat and the bagged lunch, his hands going up to his face. Claw marks ran down both cheeks. "What the—?"

The owl flew at Roger, talons latching onto his arm, beak pecking at his shoulder. The opossum sauntered up and bit him on the ankle. The duck flew up, landed on his head, and tried to pull out his hair. Roger turned around and ran away, waving the birds off. "Get away from me!" The opossum let go after a couple of steps.

Travis stood, stunned. He smiled as he scooped up the stuffed animals, now still and entirely normal looking, back into his backpack along with his lunch and water bottle.

"Those are some toys you've got there."

Travis spun around. A girl he recognized from the neighborhood peered at him curiously. Older than him by a couple of years, she stood at least a foot taller.

"Oh. You saw that?" Travis put his hand on the back of his neck.

She nodded. "Uh-huh. So," she walked closer, "how do they work?"

He thought fast. "Batteries."

She crossed her arms. "No battery could make a cat grow claws and scratch a person on its own, or have a bird fly at someone and peck them or have … " Her voice trailed off as she pointed. "What was that?"

"An opossum."

"Right, a possum bite his leg."

"Not a possum, an opossum," Travis said.

She peered at him quizzically.

Oops, he'd just gone into nerd territory. "Look, I'm gonna be late for school." He slung his bag over his shoulder and walked away.

Seconds later, the girl caught up to him. "I'll walk with you."

"You don't go to my school," he said.

She laughed. "I know that. But I do go to the middle school." Travis knew the middle school was a block down the street from his. "Name's Madison, by the way."

"Travis." He glanced at her out of the corner of his eye.

They continued half a block in silence. "Who was that kid, anyways?"

"Who?" He looked at her. "Roger?" He turned away. "A bully."

"Wait. He's a fifth grader?"

"Yep."

"Well, I'm glad your stuffies chased him away, however they did it." She stopped and touched his arm. Her eyes shone with excitement. "Are they magical?"

Travis tried to scoff but wasn't sure he pulled it off. "There's no such thing as magic."

"Yeah, you're probably right. But it would be so cool if there was." They continued walking and a moment later reached the elementary school. "Hey, if they are magical, like really magical, will you tell me? I can keep a secret."

He considered her request. Madison seemed nice and hadn't laughed at him for having stuffed animals in his backpack. She also seemed really excited at the idea of magic. "Sure."

"Sure, they're magical, or sure, you'll tell me if they are?"

Travis laughed. "Sure, I'll tell you if they are."

"Cool. See ya around then."

"See ya." He turned and headed into school.

***

The day proved to be unremarkable as school days go. Social studies was interesting—they watched a documentary about indigenous peoples of the United States—math was confusing—fractions again—and then came recess. Throughout the day, Roger stayed clear of him. Though Travis did catch the bully watching him out of the corner of his eye. In fact, Roger seemed to stay clear of everyone, and there was a noticeable change in the energy in the yard. In a good way.

Travis meant to show Marcus his animals during recess, but he'd left his backpack in the classroom and couldn't figure out how to bring up the subject without sounding stupid. At lunch, Marcus went into elaborate detail about his new video game, and Travis forgot all about what was in his bag. By the end of the day, he couldn't bring himself to mention the stuffed animals, because he feared Marcus would laugh at him.

Chapter 4

Madison surprised Travis as he walked out of school. She stood leaning against a tree, waiting for him. "Hey, wait up," she called out as he passed.

He stopped. "I thought middle school got out later."

"I have a free period on Friday afternoons. So, gonna tell me?"

"Tell you what?"

"About these animals. How you got them, and what makes them magical?"

"I never said—"

"Come on," she interrupted. "I saw what they did to that bully. Those are no ordinary stuffed animals."

Travis walked in silence. Finally he said, "Promise you won't laugh."

"Laugh? At what? At you?"

Travis shrugged.

"Why would I laugh at you?"

"'Cause I'm a fifth grader with a bag full of stuffed animals."

"No. You're a fifth grader with a bagful of magical awesomeness that took down a school bully."

Travis couldn't help himself. He smiled. "Okay," he said, nodding and continuing down the block.

"Okay, what?"

He sensed her watching him, but he kept his gaze forward. "Okay, I'll tell you. Only, you have to swear not to tell anyone."

"I already told you I can keep a secret."

He jumped over a crack in the sidewalk, turned, and blocked Madison's path. "You have to swear it."

The corner of her mouth turned up. "Okay. I swear I will not tell a living soul about what's in your backpack or anything about them. Is that good enough?"

Travis stepped aside, and they walked together down the street. "Yep. That's good enough." He jumped over a branch lying in his path. "Can you come over to my house?"

"Sure. You mean, like, now?"

"Yes, now."

"Okay."

They covered the short walk in silence. Once they reached his house, Travis froze, his hand on the front door. "Wait."

"What?"

"I'm not supposed to let anyone into the house when my parents aren't here."

"Oh. Well, could we hang out here on the porch?"

He smiled and nodded. "Let me grab us something to eat." Unlocking the front door, he went inside.

Madison called out from the doorway. "Can I use your phone to call my mom? I'm supposed to let her know where I am."

"Sure," he yelled back without hesitation. Mom would understand another kid needing to use the phone.

Travis scoured the cupboards for something to eat, while Madison used the phone. Halfway out of the kitchen with his arms full of snacks, he froze. He dropped the food on the kitchen counter before turning to Madison. "Hold on a sec. I'll be right back." He ran down the hall to his bedroom. Baako was perched on the windowsill, facing the street. Travis grabbed her and ran back to the kitchen.

Madison caught sight of the eagle. "Another one?"

"Yeah," is all he said as he led her back outside, carrying pretzels and apples. "Sorry, my mom doesn't let me have soda. Well, sometimes she does but only on movie nights and …" His voice trailed off, seeing the look of amusement on Madison's face. He suddenly felt stupid. "Never mind. Here." He thrust the bag of pretzels at her.

She put it aside. "Can I see the animals?"

Travis glanced up and down the street. A front garden separated the porch from the sidewalk. Even if someone walked by, they wouldn't be able to see much. Having put Baako down, he unzipped his bag and took out the owl, cat, duck, and opossum and placed them next to the eagle. Set on a wooden table, they seemed like ordinary stuffed animals. The two kids sat down and waited for something to happen. Madison missed her seat, landing on the ground. She'd tried to sit without taking her eyes off the animals.

"Can I hold one?" Madison asked, getting up, nonplussed that she'd missed the chair.

"Sure. Though you might want to be careful with the cat."

Madison chuckled, choosing the owl. She turned it over in her hands before replacing it on the table.

"Baako, this is Madison."

The eagle didn't move. Madison stared at Travis. "Who's Baako?"

Travis pointed to the eagle. "She was the first. Baako, Madison watched the others attack a bully today. She knows."

He focused on the eagle. Out of the corner of his eye, he noticed Madison holding her breath. She inched forward in her seat.

Baako rustled her feathers, signaling the others. The cat stretched, the owl blinked, the duck flapped its wings, and the opossum rolled over and played dead.

"Wow." It came out in a whisper as Madison fell onto her knees in front of the animals. "Who are you?"

The eagle turned to her. "I am Baako, the original magic buddy."

"A magic what?" Travis said. "You didn't tell me that's what you're called."

Baako swiveled her head back and forth between the two kids. "I didn't know you came in different colors."

"What?" Baako's reference to their skin color—Travis was Black, Madison, white—took both kids off guard.

"I sense in her," Baako said, still staring at Madison, "a certain ability. I think she will make a good detective. But why does she have no color? Is she the only one?"

Travis and Madison glanced at each other and burst out laughing.

"I do not understand what is so funny," Baako said.

"Never mind," Madison said, still chuckling.

"What did you mean about her being a good detective?" Travis asked. "Why didn't you tell me these things?"

"Everything in its own time," Baako said. "Now the others—"

"—where did they come from?" Madison interrupted.

"They came from Baako," Travis said quickly before Baako could answer. He told her what had happened in his room the night before.

"And what are their names?" Madison asked.

"Who cares? I want to know what powers they have and why she," he pointed to Baako, "came to me. And who dropped her on my front porch?"

"They don't come with names," Baako said.

"Oh! Can I name them?" Madison asked. Her eyes sparkled, and she scooted to the edge of her chair.

"Sure." It didn't matter to Travis until …

"Kitty. The cat's name is Kitty."

"No, it's not." Travis countered.

"What's wrong with Kitty?"

Travis watched the cat lick its stomach. "Too girly."

"Okay, you name it."

He shook his head. "No, go ahead. Just not that."

Madison glared at him before turning to the cat, now licking one of its front paws. "How about Killer? Since she tried to kill that bully."

"Awesome!"

"I was only kidding."

"Oh."

"Tiger." Madison nodded. "Yeah, that's it. See how she's got some black side markings that aren't quite stripes but combined with her orange body, I'd say she kind've looks like one. Plus, she's ferocious enough." The cat rolled on its side, eyes closed.

Travis agreed. "Alright. Tiger." He leaned forward in his wooden chair. "Who's next?"

"The owl." They both turned their attention to the bird, standing still as if it really were simply a stuffed animal.

"He almost took Roger's eye out," Travis said. "How about Eyeball?" The owl's eyes shot open.

Madison gawked at him. "You're kidding, right? Please tell me you're kidding."

"Yeah, sure, I'm kidding." Flustered by his blushing, he turned and pretended to be interested in a car driving down the street. "How about Bully Buster?"

"No."

"Bully Beater?" The corner of his mouth turned up.

"No."

"Bully Eyeball Buster?" He grinned.

"No!" Madison turned to face Travis. He burst out laughing. She joined in.

"Fine," he said. "You choose."

"How about Woodstock?" she suggested.

He tilted his head. "Huh?"

"You know, Woodstock. From Snoopy?"

"Oh. He doesn't look anything like Woodstock." He stared at the bird for a moment. "But, okay."

"Oh, thank goodness," the owl said, sounding as if he'd just sucked in a balloon filled with helium. Madison whipped around to stare at the raptor while Travis's jaw dropped. "What?" the owl continued. "Wouldn't you be relieved if you'd escaped being named Bully Eyeball Buster?"

Madison stared at Travis. "They can all …"

"Talk." He finished her sentence.

"Of course we can talk," Tiger said, without opening her eyes. Her voice reminded Travis of his grandmother when she was giving him a lecture.

"What did you expect?" Woodstock said. "That only Baako had that power?"

"So why am I the last to get a name?" a gruff voice said. The opossum rolled off its back and onto all fours.

"Because you were playing dead?" Travis suggested apologetically.

"You're not the last." The duck pulled her head out from under her wing. "I don't have a name either." She sounded insulted.

"Oh," Travis waved his finger at the duck. "I know. Quack."

"Quack?" Madison asked.

"Quack," he insisted.

"Okay."

"So what's his name?" Travis pointed to the opossum.

"I want you to name me," the opossum said to Travis.

"Me?"

The opossum nodded.

He thought for several moments, his eyes rolling up toward the sky. A smile, small at first, grew into a wide grin. "Stiff."

Madison broke out in laughter. "You asked for it," she said to the marsupial. He didn't seem to mind.

Chapter 5

"Now that you're done with that, can we move on to more important business?" Baako asked.

"Business?" Madison said.

"Yeah," Travis said. "Baako here thinks I'm supposed to help him ward off an evil warlock."

"You mean like a witch?" Madison asked.

"Or wizard, yeah," Travis said.

"Is he coming here?" Madison asked. "Or do we have to find him?"

"Find him?" He stared at her incredulously. "Why would we want to find him?"

"Do you tend to wait for bad things to happen to you?" she asked.

"What do you mean?" he said. "Oh, like Roger? Maybe. But going after an evil whatever? What do we do? Go searching all over the city for him? Or how 'bout we get on a plane and go find him?"

"Great idea," Baako said.

"Baako," Travis said, "I'm ten years old. Madison is …" He turned to her.

"Twelve."

"Madison is twelve. We can't just get on a plane and go somewhere. I can't even drive for, like, ever." He paused for a moment. "Maybe you landed at the wrong house?"

"I never land at the wrong house." Baako sounded offended.

"What? You've done this before?" Travis asked.

The eagle ignored him. "For now, we need to devise a plan."

Madison and Travis stared at her. She stared back. After several minutes, Madison broke the silence. "Well, this is productive," she said sarcastically.

"I say we just pretend there is no warlock or witch or whatever, 'cause really, what are the chances?" Travis glanced at Madison. Her face had skepticism written all over it. "What?" he said. "What are the chances that some evil magical being exists?"

"What are the chances that magical stuffed animals exist?" Madison said.

Travis opened his mouth and then closed it again.

"Exactly." Madison peered down the street as if she expected some evil being to stroll toward the house. Instead, Travis's mom pulled into the driveway.

"Quick," Travis said. "We need to put these back in my backpack."

"Why?" Madison asked.

"Because she'll ask questions. I've never been a big stuffed animal person. Except for ... oh, never mind."

Madison smiled as she helped him put the animals back in his pack. "Except for what?"

Travis hesitated. She didn't seem to be making fun of him. "Tigger. I always liked Tigger."

"Of all the Winnie-the-Pooh characters, Eeyore's my favorite."

He smiled back at her before zipping up his bag and putting it off to the side as his mom came up the steps. "Hi, Mom."

"Hi. Who's this?" His mom smiled at Madison.

"Hi, I'm Madison," Madison said, waving.

"Hi, Madison." Turning to Travis she asked, "Why are you outside on the porch?"

"Because you said I'm not supposed to let anyone in the house."

"Right. Well, you can come inside now."

Madison followed Travis through the house and into his room. Travis turned his backpack upside down on his bed and the animals tumbled out.

"Get off me," the owl's squeaky voice said from under the opossum.

"Hold on to your feathers," Stiff said, before standing up and moving off to the side.

"Who stinks?" Woodstock asked, before smelling her own backside. Baako flapped her wings several times.

Both kids stared at the group. "What are we supposed to do now?" Travis asked.

"What if we formed a club? Yeah," Madison nodded to herself. "The eagle said we need to make a plan. So I say we form a club."

"And what would that club do, exactly?" Travis asked.

"Find this evil warlock."

"How are we going to do that?"

"Are you always so full of questions?" Madison asked.

He shrugged. "Maybe?"

"Well, how about coming up with a solution?"

Travis plopped down on his bed, picked up the owl, and turned it over absentmindedly in his hands. "Baako said that this evil person would find us, right? So let's form a club, like you said. And be ready for whoever comes." He looked up at Madison. "How's that for an idea?"

She smiled. "Great. Is there anyone you'd want to be in the club?"

"You mean someone who won't laugh at me when I ask them?" He shook his head. "Nah."

"But it's how you ask them that'll make the difference," she insisted. "Who's your best friend?"

"Marcus," he said. "And he would laugh if I told him I had a bunch of stuffed animals that came alive."

"Sure," she said dismissively. "But if instead of doing that, you showed him what they could do and then asked him, do you still think he would laugh?"

Travis considered Madison with a tilt of his head. A smile started small but spread quickly to his eyes. "No. I don't think he would." After a pause, he asked, "So, what about you? Who would you invite?"

"My best friend, Stacey. She'd be up for it, I'm sure of it."

"So that would be four of us. Do we need a fifth since there are five animals?"

They sat in silence for a minute. "Actually, no," Travis said, answering his own question. "Baako is special, being first. But each of us can take one animal. Baako stays here."

"I get to take one home?" Madison asked, clearly stunned.

"Sure. Why not?" Travis examined each of the animals in turn, trying to figure out which one he'd want. The opossum or the cat?

"Can I take Tiger?" Madison asked.

"Sure. Then I'll keep Stiff."

Madison glanced down at her watch. "Oops. I should be going. Can I take Tiger now?"

"Sure."

Madison picked up the cat and put him in her backpack. "I wonder if there's a way to clip them onto our bags. What if they change shape or color or try to talk to us but we can't tell 'cause we keep them hidden?"

Travis shrugged, having nothing to say. He walked Madison out to the front door. "See you later," he said.

"Yeah. Oh, wait." She pulled her backpack off her shoulder, took out a notebook, and scribbled something on a piece of paper. She tore it off and handed it to him. "Here's my phone number. Call me if you want to get together over the weekend."

"Sure. Thanks." He accepted the piece of paper.

After Madison left, Travis went to join his mom in the kitchen.

"Found a new friend, I see," his mom said when he found her in the kitchen.

"Yeah."

"She's not in your class, is she?"

"Nah. She's in middle school."

"How did you two meet?"

He sighed. "Remember that bully?" His mom nodded. "Well, he was giving me a bad time, and she sort of stepped in and told him to knock it off. And he did."

"Do I need to call the school about that kid?"

"No." He shook his head. "I have a feeling he'll leave me alone."

"Well, I don't like the idea of you hanging around with middle schoolers, but if she stood up for you, I'll make an exception."

"Thanks, Mom." He walked over and sniffed at a pan on the stove. "What's for dinner?"

"Food. Now go make yourself useful and set the table."

Chapter 6

When Travis arrived at school on Monday morning, he found Madison standing against a tree near the parking lot. "Oh hi, Madison."

"I thought we were going to get together this weekend," she said, a hint of anger in her voice.

"Were we?" Travis worried he'd forgotten something.

"Well, we didn't exactly plan anything. But I gave you my number and expected you'd call. I assumed you wanted to work on the club." She sounded hurt, as if there'd been a party, and she was the only one who hadn't been invited.

"I did." Bewildered by this exchange, Travis could tell that she didn't believe him. "I do," he insisted. "But my mom gave me extra chores, then I went with my dad on a bunch of errands, then I had soccer practice, my grandma came over …" his voice trailed off.

Madison seemed at least partly convinced. "Um," she said awkwardly. "Would you call me next time? Let me know if you can't get together?"

"You want me to call when I can't meet with you?" He tilted his head quizzically.

"Only if we've talked about maybe meeting up."

"Um, okay." He found the entire conversation confusing but felt that was the safest thing to say.

"Can you meet after school today?" Madison asked.

"I've already made plans with Marcus."

"Well, great. We can tell him about the club."

"Not today. We're going to the skatepark."

"You don't think this is important, do you?" The disappointment in her voice was hard to miss.

"Of course it's important. I …" Travis struggled to find the right words, afraid he would say something wrong. "I just don't think it's so important I can't hang out with my best friend."

"Okay. Well, call me when it's important enough." She turned and walked away.

Travis stood watching her for a moment before shaking his head as if to clear it of cobwebs. He turned to go into school and walked right into Marcus.

"Hey, there you are." Marcus play punched him on the shoulder. "We're gonna be late."

"Okay, I'm coming."

"Who was that?" Marcus asked as they headed into the main school building.

"A girl I met last week," Travis said. "You still up for going to the skatepark after school?"

"Yeah. Oh. Guess what? I got a new board."

"Nice. Meet at my house after school?" Travis's house was blocks from the park.

"Sure."

***

After an uneventful school day, Travis headed home, hungry for the cookies his mom brought home from the store over the weekend, but not because he'd missed lunch. This was the first Monday he could remember that Roger hadn't stolen his food or his money. Roger seemed to be staying clear of Travis, which was fine with him. He climbed the steps to his house, and before he could put his key in the door, it swung open.

"Mom?" Travis stepped into the house. Was his mom home early? A crash sounded from down the hall. It sounded like it came from his room. "Mom?" He called out, louder this time. The hairs on the back of his neck stood up. Something made him hesitate to go toward his room. Walking backwards, his stomach tightening in a knot, he made his way to the front door, turned and ran down his front steps as Marus rolled up on his skateboard.

"Hey, what's up?" Marcus asked.

"I … There's someone … um … in my house," Travis stammered.

"What? You sure?"

Travis nodded. "I don't know what to do."

"Are you sure it's not just your mom?"

He shook his head. "I called out for her, but she didn't answer. Then I heard a crash in my room. Her car's not here." Travis's eyes grew wide. "But maybe someone gave her a ride home because she was sick or something."

He raced back into the house, Marcus following close behind. Through the door, down the hall and into his room where there was … nothing. A pile of books and a jar of loose change from a shelf were now on the floor. That must have been the crash. There was nothing else amiss.

"What's with all the stuffed animals on your bed?" Baako, along with Stiff, Woodstock and Quack, were grouped together on his pillow.

"Oh, yeah." Travis stood awkwardly in the middle of his room, wondering what to say. He remembered Madison's suggestion while he took in the mess on his floor. "Did you guys do this?" he said, addressing the animals on his bed.

"Who you talking to?" Marcus asked.

"Baako. This is my best friend, Marcus, and I want him to be in the club." Out of the corner of his eye, Travis could see Marcus, confusion written on his face, turning his head between Travis and the bed. His mouth dropped open when voices broke out in a chorus of accusations.

"He did it," Quack the duck said.

"Who, me?" Stiff said. "I did not. How's an opossum gonna get up there?"

"Don't look at me," Woodstock said.

"Enough," Baako said sternly.

Marcus's helmet fell out of his hand onto the floor.

"Soooo," Travis said, drawing out the o. "That's what's with the stuffed animals. They're magical."

"Uh-huh." Marcus nodded.

"They can obviously talk."

"Uh-huh." Marcus continued to nod.

"And I'm guessing they can do other stuff, too," he finished lamely.

"Uh-huh."

Marcus stood wide-eyed in the middle of the room, nodding his head. His helmet lay on the floor at his feet.

"You okay?" Travis asked.

"Uh-huh."

"Marcus!" Travis yelled at him.

Marcus stopped nodding his head. "What?"

"You okay? Thought you were gonna nod your head off."

"Where'd you get these?" Marcus asked.

Travis told Marcus the story, trying not to leave anything out. When he finished, Travis started picking up the books and change on his floor. "What were you guys doing in here anyways?" he asked.

"He did it!" exclaimed Quack.

"Who, me?" started Stiff. "I did—"

"Guys, enough!" Travis said. "Don't go on repeating the same excuses you gave before."

"Oh, you want new ones?" Quack asked. "It wasn't me!"

"No, no, that's not what I meant!" Travis said. He ran his hand over his short black hair.

Baako cleared her throat. Everyone paused. "We didn't do this."

Travis eyed her curiously. "What do you mean?"

"He was here," Baako said, fluffing her feathers.

"Whoa," Marcus stepped back, "they can move too?"

"Of course we can move," Woodstock said.

He launched himself into the air and flew around the room, hooting. Stiff rolled over onto his back while Quack flapped her wings. Marcus put his arms over his head to protect himself.

Travis laughed so hard he bent over, grabbing his stomach. When he stopped and stood up again, he caught Baako watching him. "What?"

"He was here," Baako repeated.

"Who?" Travis asked.

"The evil warlock."

Chapter 7

Travis stared at Baako, confused. He remembered the unlocked front door. "Where is he now?"

"He jumped out the window," Baako said.

Only then did Travis realize that the screen was missing from his open window. As he stared outside, he had a sudden inspiration. Without a word, he opened his desk drawer, grabbed a piece of paper, and bolted down the hall to the kitchen. He picked up the phone and dialed. "Come on, come on." Someone picked up on the fourth ring.

"Hello?"

"Hi, can I speak to Madison?"

"Speaking."

"Hi, it's Travis."

"Oh, do—"

Travis talked over her. "I need you to come over to my house right now!"

"What? Why?"

"I just need you to—"

"I can't just drop everything and—"

"The warlock was here!" he yelled. "In my house!" He paced back and forth as far as the phone cord would let him.

"Okay. We'll be over as soon as we can."

"Who's we?" he said, but Madison hung up the phone before the words left his mouth. He dashed back to his room.

Marcus hadn't moved. He continued to stare at the bed, his mouth ajar. Woodstock was standing on Stiff's back. Quack pecked at the comforter. Tiger was licking his paws. Travis ignored Marcus and addressed the eagle.

"What was he looking for?"

"Me. Only, he didn't know that."

"What do you mean?"

"Somehow, he tracked me to this location, but he doesn't know that I am the one he seeks. He stood in the middle of the room, turning in circles. You came home not long after he arrived."

Travis ducked as the owl, having taken off from Stuff's back, zoomed by his head. He watched it for a moment. "Woodstock. Woodstock! Hey, owl!" Woodstock stopped flying and plopped onto the bed.

"Yes."

"You need to stop flying around. Whoever was in here could be outside, watching. If he sees you, he'll realize you're magical."

"Well, you're no fun," the owl pouted.

The phone rang and Travis ran to answer it. His mom wanted to tell him that she'd be home late. He remembered to ask permission to have friends over. His mom sounded relieved that he wouldn't be home alone. About to return to his room, he stopped when someone knocked on the front door. Thinking it was Madison, he opened it without checking the peephole.

Travis came face to face with a tall white man dressed all in black: black shirt, pants, shoes and hat. A goatee ended in a narrow point below his chin. His light-blue eyes were narrow and cold. As the man's mouth spread into a wicked grin, Travis tried to shut the door. The man stuck his foot in the door and pushed it open.

"You have something I want." He pushed past Travis and down the hall.

"He's coming!" Travis yelled, following the man down to his room.

The man shoved Marcus aside and grabbed Woodstock. "Got you." The other animals stayed completely still, like regular stuffed toys.

"What do you want with him?" Travis said.

"The Grand Wizard put his powers into this creature before I killed him."

"You k … k … killed …?" Marcus stuttered.

The man ignored him. "I thought his powers would become mine once I killed him, but I was mistaken." He looked greedily at Woodstock, now an unremarkable stuffed toy in his hand.

Travis's back was to his desk and window. He glanced over his shoulder, looking for a way out. When he turned back around, it was just in time to see Madison swinging a frying pan at the man's head. The man must have sensed her because he turned around, and the pan collided with his nose. He dropped Woodstock as his hands flew to his face.

A girl Travis didn't recognize lunged at the man's legs, knocking him to the ground.

"What are you doing?" Marcus said, as the man began to rise. "He'll kill us!"

Travis jumped on the man's back. The girl who came with Madison still held onto his legs. "Marcus!" Travis shouted. "Help me!" The man was on his hands and knees. Marcus remained frozen. "Marcus! Now!" Madison grabbed one of the man's arms. Marcus got the idea and grabbed his other one. With Travis sitting on him, he crashed to the floor. "Got you!" Travis said.

The man's eyes glowed red. He sneered.

A tickling sensation spread over Travis's entire body causing him to snicker. He wasn't the only one; the others started to giggle.

"What?" the man stammered. "Why aren't you screaming in pain?"

"Cover his eyes." Baako said, though she hadn't moved.

"Who said that?" the man asked.

"My beanie. Where's my—?" Travis glanced around. "There." He saw it on the floor in the corner of his room, but it was too far away to reach. "Woodstock, I need that hat in the corner."

The owl, on the floor where the man dropped him, flew over, grabbed the beanie and dropped it on the man's head, covering his face. Baako immediately began to glow, and Travis realized that covering the warlock's eyes prevented him from seeing what happened next.

The man's body grew warm. Everyone jumped off as he became too hot to touch. A moment later, the man disappeared.

"Where?"

"What?

"What just happened?"

They glanced at each other in shock. Travis turned to Baako. "Did you do that?"

Baako ruffled her feathers. "Make him disappear? No. He did that."

"So, he'll be back," Travis said.

"Perhaps not," Baako said.

"What's that supposed to mean?" Madison asked.

"I erased his memory before he disappeared," Baako said. "At least I think I did. One can never be sure about these things."

"Never be …?" Marcus couldn't quite get his words out.

Silence filled the room. Marcus and Madison were on their feet, but Madison's friend still grasped invisible legs on the floor. Travis sat on the floor where he landed once the man disappeared.

"Madison, is this Stacey?"

"Yep, I'm Stacey." She pushed herself up into a sitting position. Swiping her jet-black hair away from her eyes, she smiled at Travis as she redid her ponytail.

"Baako, everyone is here," Travis said. "Maybe you can tell us what's really going on."

"As his last act, a great wizard, created me," Baako said. "Weakened and hunted, he realized he didn't have much time."

"You weren't kidding when you said they could talk," Stacey said to Madison.

"Wait," Madison said, ignoring Stacey's comment. "Don't wizards live forever? I mean, if they're magical, why can't they?"

"I don't know." Baako said. "But he created me as a vessel for his powers, wishing his work to continue."

"What work?" Stacey asked.

Baako regarded Stacey in silence. "Fighting those who use magic to do evil in the world."

"Like what?" Stacey said.

"You have to understand, I was created mere hours before he died. There was just enough time for him to tell me to find you."

"Find me?" Travis said.

"So you don't know what weakened him?" Marcus asked at the same time, talking over Travis. "I mean, before he made you?"

Baako dropped her head. "No."

"But he was a wizard," Stacey repeated.

Baako looked up at her. "Yes, but so was the other." No one spoke for several moments. Everyone watched Baako, including the other animals huddled together on the floor.

Chapter 8

"Soon after he created me," Baako continued, "the wizard—the Grand Wizard—suffered a mortal wound inflicted by the man you saw here today. Creating me sapped him of the strength he needed to defend himself. Before his fight, he packed me away."

"So you didn't see what happened?" Marcus asked.

"No."

"Then how can you be certain he's dead?" Madison asked.

"The last words he spoke to me were, 'Find the children.' I looked into his eyes as he said those words. There was little life in them."

"But why here? Why me?" Travis asked.

"I do not know." Baako said. "I was to find others who could be trusted with magic. He told me to only confide in children."

"But how did you find me? How did you end up here, in Philadelphia, of all places?"

"There is much we don't understand about magic," Baako said. "And it doesn't matter now. What matters is what you do next."

"Let's form a club like we talked about," Madison said to Travis.

"Before we do anything, you got any snacks, Trav?" Marcus said.

Stacey and Madison turned on Marcus. "How can you think of food at a time like this?" Madison said.

"Hey," Marcus said defensively, "I'm hungry. I can't think when my stomach's talking." On cue, his stomach rumbled.

"Sure. Be back in a sec." Travis raced down the hall into the kitchen, grabbed a bag of pretzels and a six-pack of soda meant to last him a month, then darted back to his room. He passed the sodas around and opened the bag of pretzels. The four kids sat on the floor, their attention on the eagle perched on the bed.

"So," Marcus asked. "What kind of club?"

Travis opened his soda. Three other soda cans popped open, as if the others had been waiting for him. Marcus already had his hand in the pretzel bag.

"One where we go find the evil warlocks and defeat them," Madison said. She took a large gulp of soda before taking the pretzel bag from Marcus and grabbing a handful.

"How can you think of food at a time like this?" Marcus asked sarcastically.

Madison smiled.

"There you go again with finding evil warlocks thing," Travis said. "We don't have any way of going anywhere. And who are we going to defeat with a bunch of stuffed animals? What are we going to do? Talk them to death?"

"Are you sure that's all they can do?" Stacey asked. Madison, her mouth full, pointed at her as if to say, "Listen to her."

"Well," Travis said, addressing all the creatures on the bed. "Do you have other powers?"

"Do we have any?" Stiff started, clearly insulted. "Of course we have powers." He turned toward Baako. "Don't we?" he said, his voice suddenly filled with doubt.

"Not yet," Baako said. "It's not wise to give you full powers when you're so young."

"Young?" Woodstock said. "Young? How much older are you than me? Huh? Huh?"

"Perhaps the word I should have used is mature," Baako said.

The owl crossed its wings in front of its body and stomped its foot.

"I didn't know owls could do that," Stacey said.

"You want Woodstock?" Travis asked.

"What? You mean we each get one of these?"

"If you agree to be in the club," Travis said.

"Yeah, absolutely." Stacey held out her hand and Woodstock flew into her palm.

"Shouldn't we decide what this club is going to do before we form it?" Madison asked.

"Nah. Let's form it first, and then we can decide together," Travis said. "But we need to promise to keep it a secret first."

Marcus tried to talk with his mouth full of pretzels. "I'm wont bonna …" He swallowed his pretzels and took a swig of soda before speaking again. "I'm not gonna tell anyone. What would I say? 'Hey, look at my stuffed …'"

Marcus glanced at the animals on the bed. "Which one would I get? Oh, can I have the eagle?"

"No," Travis said. "The eagle stays here with me. And I'm keeping the opossum as well."

"Tiger's mine," Madison said, stroking the cat resting in her lap.

"I already called the owl," Stacey said.

Travis grinned. "So I guess you've got Quack."

Marcus smirked.

"Just as I thought," Quack said. "Nobody wants me." The duck tucked her bill and head under her feathers, like an ostrich sticking its head into a hole.

"What?" The smirk fell off Marcus's face.

The others broke out laughing. "Okay, okay," Madison said, the first to get her laughter under control. "So is it agreed that we're all in this club, and we promise to keep everything about the club secret?" The others nodded. "Great. So next, let's come up with a name."

"The Magical Creature Society," Stacey offered.

"Good." Madison nodded. "Except that it might not be a good idea to use the word magical. Just in case we're ever talking about it and someone overhears us."

"What exactly are we going to be doing in this club?" Marcus asked.

"Fighting evil wizards?" Travis shrugged before adding, "I guess?"

"But we'd have to find these wizards—" Madison said.

"—unless they find us first," Travis interrupted.

Madison ignored his interruption. "Kind've like being detectives. That's what Baako called me the other day."

"Oh, I like the sound of that," Stacey said.

"Didn't you say something earlier about traveling to wherever we needed to go, and didn't Baako agree with you?" Travis said.

"Yeah, yeah." Madison sat up eagerly. "How about The Traveling Detectives?"

"Wait," Marcus said. "How are we gonna travel?"

"Don't know. Don't care," Madison said.

"Maybe we don't have to. That wizard found us. Maybe we don't have to go looking for trouble," Travis said. "Though they did do a good job of taking down Roger," he admitted.

"What?" Marcus said, spraying pretzels at the rest of the group. As they all recoiled and complained and wiped pretzel bits off of themselves, Marcus added, "What did they do to Roger?" after taking a drink of soda.

"I'll tell you later," Travis said.

"We should have the word club in the name," Stacey said, wiping crumbs off her sleeve.

"Sure," Madison said. "But Travis, sometimes you can't just sit back and wait for trouble to find you. You need to go out and stop trouble from happening."

They sat around quietly for several minutes.

"Okay. Listen to this." Madison leaned toward the others. "How about, The Travelers Detective Club?"

Everyone was quiet for a moment. Then, one by one, they voiced their approval.

Travis nodded. "Yeah, that's good. Even if we don't go anywhere," he muttered.

Madison ignored his last remark.

"Cool," Marcus said, careful to swallow first.

"We could call it the TDC for short," Stacey added.

"Sweet," Madison said. She held up her soda, and the others followed. "Welcome to The Travelers Detective Club."

Chapter 9

Two weeks later, the new group of friends rode their bikes down to the river. While they officially lived in Philadelphia, their neighborhood was on the outskirts of the city, between Center City and the suburbs.

On the way, they passed Roger, the elementary school bully. They stared at him as they rode by, keeping space between him and themselves. He didn't look up as they rode past.

"Did anyone else notice that Roger looked like he'd been crying?" There was a hint of glee in Marcus's voice.

"Really?" Travis said. "Serves him right."

"That's not very nice," Madison said.

"Yeah, well, you don't know Roger," Travis said. "I could come to school crying about my dead sister, and he'd still steal my lunch money."

"You have a sister?" Madison said.

"No." Travis propped his bike up against a tree and made his way over large boulders of varying sizes, down to a rocky shore and the edge of the river. He picked up a round, smooth stone and threw it across the surface of the water. It skipped three times.

"Not bad." Marcus grabbed a rock, leaned sideways, and threw it across the water. It sank immediately.

"You can't throw just any old rock," Madison said, coming up from behind. "It has to be flat."

"You try," Marcus grumbled.

Madison scoured the ground, picked up a flat rock the size of a dime and threw it sidearm across the water.

"Six," Stacey said. "Nice."

They took turns throwing rocks into the river as the sun rose high in the sky.

"Um, guys," Marcus said, "I think there's someone watching us."

"Where?" They all turned to follow his gaze, focused up in the trees near where they'd left their bikes.

"Who's there?" Stacey called out.

"What are you doing?" hissed Marcus, taking a step backwards.

Stacey called over her shoulder to Marcus. "It's fine." She walked forward until she came to the first boulder. Scrambling on top of it, she called out again. "I see you hiding behind the tree."

Whether she actually spotted someone or was bluffing wasn't clear to the others, but emboldened by her action, they climbed up onto adjacent boulders.

Roger stepped out from behind a tree. His face held an expression somewhere between embarrassment and anger.

"You!" Travis called out. "What are you doing here?" His voice seethed with accusation and dislike.

"Travis!" Madison admonished.

"What?" Travis said.

Any embarrassment that may have been on Roger's face disappeared, replaced with malice. He stared at Travis momentarily, then he turned to the bikes. The corner of his mouth turned up. He turned back to Travis. "Bike shopping." He stood ten feet from the bikes while the others were at least thirty feet away, half the distance made up of a field of boulders.

Roger sauntered over to the bike nearest him, which happened to be Travis's, pulled it away from the tree and sat on it.

"Hey!" the others chorused.

Madison and Stacey, perhaps because they were the oldest or the bravest or both, moved first. They scrambled across the boulders. Travis and Marcus took their cue and followed, though not feeling all that brave. They had, after all, been on the receiving end of Roger's bullying.

As the others ran toward him, Roger snickered and took off on Travis's bike. Madison reached her bike first. Not waiting for the others, she rode off after Roger, with Stacey right behind her. Marcus was several steps behind. Once at his bike, he glanced at Travis.

"Go!" Travis said as he took off running. Marcus quickly passed him. Rounding a corner, Travis spotted Madison and Stacey stopped at the end of the lane. As he got closer, Travis noticed his bike on the ground between them and slowed to a walk. "What happened?"

Stacey straddled her bike; one foot on the ground and her left foot on her pedal. "We were chasing him and he kept looking back and probably realized he couldn't lose us, so he ditched the bike and ran off through the woods."

"Why'd you snap at him like that?" Madison asked Travis.

"'Cause he's never up to no good, is why. And he was spying on us."

"Any chance he could have been curious about what we were doing? Even possibly want to join us?" Madison asked.

"Join us?" Travis scoffed.

"You must be kidding," Marcus added. "Roger gets enjoyment from torturing anyone smaller than him."

"Torturing?" Stacey said. "Aren't you exaggerating a little?"

"You know those hooks outside classrooms they use for hanging backpacks?" Marcus asked. The girls nodded. "He hung a first grader on one of those by the back of his underwear. If that's not torture, I don't know what is."

Travis picked up his bike. "And remember last year, when he stole that kid's lunch money and emptied his backpack in the toilet?"

Marcus nodded.

"Okay, that does sound bad," Madison acknowledged. "But why do you get so mad at him? What's he done to you?"

"That first grader was me," Travis said.

"And I had to get a new backpack," Marcus said.

"Oh," Madison said.

"Now do you get it?" Travis said.

"Yeah. It's just …" Madison's voice trailed off.

"It's just what?" Travis asked.

Madison turned to Stacey. "Did you have to go to that presentation on bullying?"

"You mean the one in 5th grade?" Stacey asked. "Yeah. But didn't you have to?" she asked the boys.

"Yeah," Marcus said. "Bullying is bad. And we're not bullies. The end."

Stacey smirked at him. "I never said you were," she said. "But why is someone like Roger a bully?"

Both boys shrugged.

"Because he's mean," Travis said.

"Yeah, but why is he mean?" Stacey asked.

"Do you think he just woke up one day and decided to be mean?" Madison asked.

"Probably," Travis said.

It was Madison's turn to smirk. "Really? Would you wake up one day and suddenly decide you wanted to beat people up?"

"No, of course not."

"If he's mean," Stacey said, "it's probably because someone is mean to him."

"Do you know anything about him?" Madison asked.

"No, and I don't want to." Travis got on his bike and pedaled down the path.

"Travis, wait up." Marcus came after him on his bike. Travis slowed down to let him catch up.

"Are they coming, too?" Travis asked.

Marcus glanced over his shoulder. "No." They pedaled side by side until they got to the end of the street, where they stopped. "Wanna come over to my house?"

"Sure."

They rode their bikes in silence for five minutes. They were almost at Marcus's house when Travis skidded to a stop and put his arm out in front of Marcus, who trailed behind.

"What?" Marcus said, stopping inches past Travis.

"Look." Travis pointed off to his left, where two figures were visible standing off to the side of an old abandoned building. "Who's that with Roger?"

"Huh?" Marcus squinted. "I can't tell. They're too far away. Why do you care?"

Travis shrugged. "If it's Roger, they must be up to no good."

The person with Roger towered over him. Even from the distance, it was clear this person, an adult, was angry. He pointed at Roger and as the man's voice rose, an occasional word could be heard by Travis and Marcus. "Stupid," and "idiot," and "why are you always …" and "can't you be more like …" shot across the distance like an arrow piercing its target. Roger hung his head and turned away. When he looked up, it was toward the two boys on their bicycles.

"Come on," Marcus said. "Let's get out of here."

Travis glanced at Roger one more time, their eyes meeting across the expansive distance.

They rode the rest of the way to Marcus's house in silence. Travis kept looking over his shoulder. A wave of goosebumps erupted over his body, and he kept thinking that Roger was following them.

Chapter 10

The next day at school, Travis grabbed a basketball from the equipment shed to play hoops before the first bell of the day rang. As he turned away with his ball, he came face-to-face with Roger.

"Were you spying on me?"

"When?"

"You know when," Roger said. "Yesterday."

"No. Why would I do that?" Travis said, taking a step back.

"If you tell anyone what you saw, I'll do more than hang you by your underwear." Roger snatched the ball away. "Got it?"

"Yeah, I got it." Feeling a flicker of bravery, Travis asked, "Can I have my ball back?"

Roger looked at him. "No." He turned, taking several steps before kicking the ball over the fence. It rolled across the street. The ball would remain there until someone threw it back over; the kids weren't allowed to go over the fence.

"Why do you have to be so mean?" Travis wasn't sure what made him say it. Possibly having new, older friends and being part of a club.

Roger froze midstep, pivoted and strode two steps to stand an inch from Travis, who had to crane his neck to look Roger in the eye.

To Travis, Roger's eyes seemed to be on fire. He quickly looked down at the ground, waiting for whatever would come next. When nothing happened, he stole a glance up at Roger. The large fifth grader seemed to be struggling to find his next words.

Travis thought about saying something but decided to take the opportunity to get away before Roger decided he'd make a good punching bag. He found Marcus hanging out with some other boys in their class on the edge of the playground. Travis joined the group but didn't take part in their banter.

He watched Roger out of the corner of his eye. Initially, the bully hung out by himself, occasionally knocking into smaller students, because with Roger, everyone was a target. Travis watched closely as Roger wandered over to the chain-link fence separating the school from the sidewalk.

A tall man in dark clothing and wearing sunglasses engaged the large fifth grader. They appeared to have a conversation through the diamond shaped holes in the fence. Roger glanced over his shoulder at Travis's group. Travis immediately dropped his gaze and pretended to pay attention to something one of the other boys said. When he glanced over in Roger's direction again, both Roger and the man had disappeared.

Who was that mysterious man? The bell rang. Travis grabbed his backpack and made his way over to his class, where he lined up with everyone else. He glanced over his shoulder to make sure Roger wasn't about to knock him from behind. There was no sign of him. The second bell rang and Mr. Burt, his fifth-grade teacher, opened the door.

Never a fan of school, Travis actually liked his teacher, most of the time, and had to admit he made learning fun. An aquarium and numerous terrariums lined up under a wall of windows on one side of the room. The class didn't have just one pet but several. Alabaster the gopher snake, Petunia the hamster, Jupiter the gecko and numerous fish, the names of which Travis refused to memorize. He didn't like any of the names except for Jupiter, which had been his idea.

Everyone found their seats, and the room quieted down as Mr. Burt stood in front of the room. Their teacher welcomed his class and was in the middle of discussing the plan for the day when the door opened and Roger ambled in.

"You're late," Mr. Burt said.

Roger didn't respond but went quietly to his seat.

Where's he been? Travis wondered. He didn't realize he was staring at Roger until Roger smirked at him and Mr. Burt called his name.

"Travis, turn around."

Travis swung around in his seat, but his mind whirled. Why did Roger seem so smug? Travis wracked his brain for answers but came up empty. His teacher pulled out his electric guitar, making Travis forget about Roger. Having a teacher who played electric guitar and taught them songs was not only cool, it got the class out of weekly choir sessions.

***

When Travis arrived home from school, both his mom and dad were home. His mom usually didn't get home until after four-thirty and his dad after six.

"Hi, Mom. Hi, Dad." Travis dropped his backpack on the floor by the front door. "You're home early. I thought you had a meeting this afternoon." He knew something was wrong when his mom didn't immediately remind him to "put it"—meaning his backpack—"where it belongs."

His parents exchanged a look. His mom gave his dad the slightest of nods. "Son," his dad said, "someone may have broken into our house."

"Oh? Wait. May have? What's that supposed to mean?"

"I came home early from work and the front door was open," his mom said. "So I called your father."

"I just got home a couple of minutes ago," Travis's dad said. "It doesn't appear as if anything was taken, so there is a possibility the door wasn't closed properly."

A jolt of electricity coursed through Travis's body. He bolted down the hallway to his room, afraid of what he wouldn't find. After a first glance, the bottom dropped out of his stomach. He didn't see Baako. His eyes frantically searched his room a second time. When they came up empty, he pulled the cover off his bed, searched under it and was in the process of pulling his action figures out of their bin when his parents came to his doorway.

"Travis," his mom asked. "What are you doing?"

"Looking for …," he found Baako at the bottom of the bin—*how did she get there*—and pulled her out. "... this."

"Sweetie," his mom said, "I know your toys are important to you, but I don't think we need to worry about someone stealing them."

Travis smiled at his parents. They turned and left. Once they were gone, Travis continued to tear his room apart because he couldn't find Stiff. He searched his room three times before he admitted defeat.

"He took Stiff, didn't he?" Travis spoke to Baako. The eagle stood on the bed where Travis placed him while looking for the opossum.

Baako didn't answer.

"What? You not talking to me now?"

Still no answer.

"Why are you ignoring me?"

Travis started toward Baako but heard a sound coming from the hallway. He stepped out to investigate and found his parents standing right outside his door.

Chapter 11

"Are you … spying on me?"

"No," his mom said. His dad shook his head.

"Well, why are you standing outside my room?"

"We came back to make sure you're okay, son."

"Why wouldn't I be okay, Dad?"

"You seemed shook up about someone breaking into the house."

"No," Travis shook his head, "I'm good. Actually, can I go to Marcus's house?"

His parents exchanged a glance. "How much homework do you have?"

"Not much. I can finish it after dinner."

"Sure, honey," his mom said. "Just be back for dinner."

"Thanks." Travis took off down the hall, past his parents, out the front door and onto his bike. He made the trip in record time—under five minutes. He dropped his bike on the ground outside the front porch, hustled up the three stairs, and knocked on the door.

Mrs. Roberts answered the door. "Oh, hi Travis. Marcus is in his room."

"Thanks Mrs. Roberts." Travis did his best not to run down the hall as Mrs. Roberts was very strict about her no running in the house policy. He succeeded, but barely. Travis burst through Marcus's bedroom door which was ajar.

Marcus was sitting on his bed listening to music on his headphones. It was a song Travis didn't know but could almost hear well enough to make out the lyrics.

"What is that?" Travis said.

"What?" Marcus said, taking off his headphones.

Travis shook his head, reminding himself of why he was there. "Never mind. Someone broke into my house, and I'm pretty sure it was that evil wizard."

"How you figure that?"

"Stiff is missing."

"Dang. You sure."

"I've searched my room three times."

"Dang."

"Is that all you've got to say?"

"What do you want me to say?"

Travis sat down on the floor and leaned against the wall opposite Marcus's bed. Pictures of Michael Jordan in all forms of play covered the wall: flying through the air to dunk the ball, spinning in the air under the basket, his tongue hanging out, standing and holding a championship trophy over his head. It didn't matter that he'd retired a long time ago and was probably an old man. Marcus idolized him.

"I don't know," Travis said, resigned.

"I thought that eagle did something to his memory."

"Maybe it didn't work."

"How'd he know to take Stiff?"

"Huh?" Travis had been staring down at the floor. He looked up when Marcus spoke.

"I said, How'd he know to take Stiff?"

"I don't know."

"Did he take any of your Tiggers?"

Travis shook his head. "No."

"So how'd he know which animal to take?"

"I said, 'I. Don't. Know.'" Travis raised his voice with each word. Travis hung his head, frustrated. When he looked up again, Marcus had his eyes closed and headphones on with his music turned up a notch. Travis got up on Marcus's bed and sat next to him.

"I'm sorry."

Marcus didn't acknowledge him.

Travis pulled the headphones away from Marcus's ear. "I'm sorry."

"You didn't need to yell."

"I know. I'm sorry. I got frustrated."

"It's an important question, you know."

"What?" Travis asked.

"How did he know to take Stiff? I mean, you do have those stuffed Tiggers. Hey," Marcus turned to look at Travis. "Did he take the eagle?"

Travis shook his head.

"You don't think Madison or Stacey would have told?"

"No way."

"Yeah, I didn't think so," Marcus said. "Well, somebody told him."

"Wait a second." Travis jumped off the bed and stood facing Marcus. "I saw Roger talking to a tall man in a dark jacket and glasses through the fence at school today. What if that man is actually the evil wizard. Roger came in late to class and made a face at me when he came in."

"How would Roger know which animals were magical?"

"Remember? They attacked Roger that one time. Didn't I tell you?"

"No, you never told me. What happened?"

Travis launched into the story, doing his best to leave nothing out.

"Oh," Marcus said. "I so wish I had been there to see that."

"So if Roger told him that I had all the animals, he was probably surprised to only find one."

"Do you think he wants all of them?" Marcus asked.

"Don't know. Maybe. But why?"

Marcus shrugged. "Ask the eagle."

Travis grabbed a Rubix Cube off the floor and fiddled with it. Not taking his eyes off of the toy, nor stopping his hands, he broke the silence first. "Marcus."

"Yeah."

"If you were the evil wizard, what would you do?"

Almost immediately, Marcus said, "Use my powers to have a lifetime supply of pizza."

"That's not what I meant."

"Oh."

"I mean, what would you do next, after finding Stiff at my house but not the other animals?"

"I'd probably follow you. Hope you'd lead me to them."

Travis and Marcus looked at each other. "Oh, no!" they chorused.

"We need to go find Madison," Travis said, standing up and walking circles in the room.

"What? No. If he followed you here, he'd follow you there."

"But I need to talk to her."

"Call her then."

"I don't know her phone number." Travis changed the direction of his circle. "Maybe we should go to my house? I have Madison's number written down, and Baako is there. We could ask one of them would what to do."

"Okay. But we need to sneak out so he doesn't spot us," Marcus said.

"Right." Travis stopped in the middle of the room. "How we gonna do that?"

"Let's go out the back door." Marcus got up off his bed, dropped his headphones and music player on the comforter and headed out his bedroom door, with Travis on his heels. Marcus twisted to face Travis as he kept walking forward, putting his index finger to his lips. Travis didn't need to be told to be quiet. They made it down the hall, through the living room and into the kitchen. Marcus had his hand on the doorknob, when—

"Where do you think you're going, young man?" Marcus's mom stood in the corner of the kitchen, her back to them, making fried chicken.

Marcus froze. "Um … we were heading over to Travis's house."

"Without asking permission?" His mom's voice sliced through the air like a knife through butter. She turned to face them.

Marcus gulped. "May I go over to Travis's house?"

"Not now. It's almost dinnertime. And I expect it's almost yours, too," she said to Travis.

"Yes, Ma'am. I'll see you tomorrow, Marcus."

"Okay. Yeah. See you tomorrow."

"Son," Mrs. Roberts said, "isn't your bike out front?"

"Oh, right." Travis turned and walked back through the house to the front door. "Maybe hide Quack somewhere," Travis whispered to Marcus before opening the door.

Marcus nodded and closed the door behind him.

Travis scanned the area but didn't notice anyone or anything out of the ordinary. Of course, if someone was good at hiding, he probably wouldn't see them anyway. He climbed on his bike and rode home, looking over his shoulder every block.

Chapter 12

The next day, on the playground before school, Travis found Marcus wide-eyed and close to tears.

"What's wrong?" Travis asked his best friend.

"Roger, that's what's wrong."

"What'd he do this time?"

"Stole my backpack. Dumped it upside down in a puddle. Look at my homework." Marcus pulled out a folder that was sopping wet.

"Go tell the teacher what happened."

Marcus shook his head. "Nah. If I did that, Roger would beat me up."

"Maybe. But maybe not."

"I don't like them odds."

"I'll come with you," Travis said. "I'll even tell the teacher about what he did to me in first grade. Someone has to stop him."

"You'd really tell about first grade?"

"Yep. I'm tired of letting Roger make me feel bad. I didn't do anything wrong. And neither did you."

"Thanks."

"You didn't have Quack in your backpack, did you?"

"No. I hid her like you said."

"Where?"

"In the fridge."

Travis laughed. "The what?"

Marcus pushed Travis on the shoulder. "You heard me. If anyone comes looking for him, they won't go there."

For Travis, the school day dragged. He got in trouble for not paying attention—he couldn't stop worrying about the evil wizard and also wanted to come up with a better villain name. The only thing he could think of was E.W.— Marcus didn't tell the teacher about Roger, instead saying he forgot his homework, which landed him in trouble as well.

After school, Marcus and Travis walked to Marcus's house together, both with slow steps and heads down, not saying much.

Mrs. Roberts welcomed them as they came through the door. "Hi, boys. I've just got back from the store. Help me bring in the rest of the groceries, will you."

The boys backtracked to the car and grabbed the remaining two bags, bringing them into the house.

"Oh, Mom. Can we take this back to my room?" Marcus held up a bag of ranch-flavored chips.

"Sure, honey. Just take some napkins with you. I don't want you wiping your fingers on your clothes."

Marcus took the bag and headed to his room, with Travis right behind. They were halfway down the hall when Mrs. Roberts' voice caught up with them. "Marcus. What is this doing in the fridge?"

"Oops." Marcus smiled at Travis and returned to the kitchen while Travis went on to his bedroom.

Travis walked into Marcus's bedroom, stepping over clothes and books on his floor to get to the bed where he plopped down.

Marcus appeared in the doorway, Quack in his arms, and froze. "What happened to my room?"

"What do you mean?"

"Someone's been through my stuff."

"Oh," Travis said. "I thought you'd just been in a rush to get to school."

"Marcus!" his mom shouted. "Get back here!"

"Uh-oh." Marcus threw Quack on the bed and walked out the door. Travis was curious, but stayed where he was. Marcus came back minutes later. Travis looked up when he entered.

"Mom wanted to know why there was food splattered all over the fridge. How would I ...?" He looked at Quack. "Quack, what did you do? Did you make that mess?"

The duck lay motionless on its side, just another stuffed animal.

"Jeez," Marcus said.

"Hey," Travis said, "do you think you know who came looking for Quack?"

"You know who?"

"E.W."

"Who?"

"The Evil Wizard."

"Oh." Marcus's eyes widened. "Oh. That would mean he did follow you the other day."

"We need to come up with a plan," Travis said.

"What kind of plan?"

"I have no idea. We need the girls' help."

***

When Travis got home that night, he called Madison and made plans to meet the next day, Friday, after school.

"I think we should bring our buddies," Madison said.

"Ok. I'll bring Baako. But what if Roger tries to steal him?"

"After what happened last time, do you really think Roger is going to steal your backpack? Besides, the wizard already stole Stiff. He doesn't know you have another buddy."

***

After an uneventful school day, Travis and Marcus met Madison across the street from their school.

"Where's Stacey?" Marcus asked.

"She's still in school. She doesn't have a free period like I do. She'll meet us later."

"Uh oh," Travis said. "Look."

The others turned to follow his gaze. Roger was across the street, staring at them.

"Let's get out of here," Marcus said.

"Wait." Madison checked for traffic before heading across the street.

"What are you doing?" Travis yelled after her.

Madison kept going. Travis and Marcus stood watching as she approached Roger. Madison clearly asked Roger something, but they were too far away to hear. Madison looked back at them and Roger did as well. A moment later, Roger shook his head. Madison made her way back across the street.

"What—?"

"I invited him to hang out with us."

"You what?" the boys chorused.

"He clearly doesn't have any friends."

"He's working with E.W.," Travis said, his voice dripping with accusation.

Madison looked at Travis, confused.

"That guy. The Evil Wizard. I couldn't think of another name," he added lamely. "Anyways, Roger is working with him."

"Because he has no friends," Madison said.

The three of them looked across the road at Roger, who faced their way, probably watching them. As they stared, he turned and walked away.

"Let's get out of here," Travis said.

"Where to?" Madison asked.

"I was hoping you had an idea," Travis said.

"You said that the evil … that E.W. followed you, right?" she asked Travis.

"I think so."

"Then we need to split up. Remember the place by the river where we hung out last week?"

The boys nodded.

"Meet me there in thirty minutes."

"How we gonna get there in thirty minutes?" Marcus asked.

"Ride your bike," Madison said.

"Oh, yeah. And we can use them to make a fast getaway if E.W. shows up."

"You're going to outrace a magician on your bike?" Travis asked incredulously.

"It could happen," Marcus said defensively.

Chapter 13

Thirty minutes later, the three sat at the river's edge, their bikes stashed in the trees at various intervals. Madison insisted they spread the bikes out. Baako, Quack and Tiger rested on the sand, the kids sitting cross-legged nearby.

Travis turned to Madison to ask her a question. But at that moment, Marcus picked Tiger up in his hand and launched the cat into a pretend attack on Quack, distracting Travis. With difficulty, Travis ignored Marcus.

"What's your plan?" he asked Madison.

"I don't have one, exactly." Travis opened his mouth to complain, but Madison spoke first. "And before you say anything, it doesn't seem like you have a plan either."

Travis closed his mouth.

"How about you plan to hand those over to me." E.W. stepped out from behind a tree. Dressed in black from head to toe, including his glasses, which reflected the sun off its mirrored surface, his presence sent a chill through the group. A group of boulders and several feet of sand were all that separated the kids from the wizard.

"I can't believe you were dumb enough to come to this same spot." He made a show of shaking his head, chuckling as he did so. "Well, no, I can. Believe you were so dumb, that is. Kids are so predictable. Not an ounce of common sense in them."

Out of the corner of his eye, Travis noticed that Baako was glowing. He moved in front of the eagle, motioning for the others to move close together, thereby blocking the buddies from E.W.'s view.

"What do we do?" Marcus whispered. The wizard had reached the boulders and stepped up onto the first.

Travis spotted Madison put one hand behind her back, palm up. Tiger jumped into her hand. Travis nudged Marcus on his left and when E.W. looked down to place his foot, Travis put his hand behind his back. Marcus got the hint and did the same. Quack jumped into Marcus's hand and Baako jumped into Travis's.

"On the count of three," Madison said, "split up and head for the bikes."

"One." E.W. stepped across the first set of boulders.

"Two." The wizard approached the halfway point. Five more boulders, and he'd reach them.

"Three." The kids bolted from their spot. Marcus and Travis going left, Madison right. They ran down the beach before turning and heading across the boulders. E.W. continued toward the beach until he realized the kids split and turned around, giving him a head start across the rocks.

Marcus made it across first, racing to his bike. On Travis's right, Madison cleared the boulders and headed for her bike. As Travis looked at Madison, his foot slipped, and he went down. He could hear E.W. scrambling toward him. Baako lay on the ground where Travis dropped her. "Baako, go."

The eagle blinked before taking flight. Travis stood up. A motion caught his attention, and he saw E.W. raise his arm, a wand in his hand, and point it at Baako. Travis turned, took a step and pushed the wizard as hard as he could. Now normally a ten-year-old boy wouldn't be able to push a grown man down, but the wizard was standing with each foot on a separate boulder, his arm outstretched and his attention toward the sky.

After Travis pushed him, E.W.'s arms windmilled in the air, trying to keep himself from falling. But fall he did. Having twisted himself part way around, he put his arms out to stop himself, landing on his side. Travis watched him for a second before remembering he should be running away and tore off toward his bike.

When he reached it, Baako was perched on his handlebars. As Travis grabbed his bike from where it leaned against a tree, Baako spoke. "Wait."

"Wait? Are you crazy?" But as he said this, Travis looked back toward the boulders. Something flashed in the sky. "What the heck?" Travis squinted. "Is that?" He couldn't believe what he was seeing. Quack was flying through the air with Tiger on her back.

At the exact moment he determined his mind wasn't playing tricks on him, Tiger jumped from Quack's back, still fifteen feet in the air, and seemed to float down toward the ground. Something flashed out of Quack's eyes.

"Is she shooting lasers?" Travis exclaimed. "From her eyes?"

Unfortunately, Quack hit Tiger when the cat touched the ground, freezing her the moment her paws met a boulder. Quack seemed to panic. She spun around in the air, shafts of red light shooting from her eyes. Tree branches were sliced from trees, a crow, flying by, froze in midair and plummeted to the ground.

"Oh my," was all Baako said.

At that moment, Stacey rolled up on her bike. "What's going—?"

"I need Woodstock," Baako interrupted.

"Okay," Stacey said, clearly confused. She pulled the owl out of her pocket and held him in the palm of her hand.

Baako glowed as she'd done back on the beach. Woodstock did the same. "We need the wand," Baako said. "And Tiger."

"Got it." Woodstock took flight.

"What should we do?" Travis asked.

"Nothing."

"Nothing?"

"He is a wizard with a wand. A weakened one for sure, but still a wizard. You have no magic."

"No. But surely I can do something."

"Yes, we need to help." Madison skidded her bike next to Stacey. Marcus stopped right behind her.

"If you can give them magic," Stacey said, "does that mean you can give it to us, too?"

"No." Baako's voice was firm, decisive.

"Why not?" Marcus said.

Quack was zigzagging through the air, clearly not trusting herself to use her powers beyond that of flight. Woodstock dive bombed the wizard, who countered with bursts of light from his wand.

"They clearly need our help," Travis said.

"You'll need to use what you already have," Baako said.

"We don't have anything," Marcus countered.

"Surely you have your brains. Work together. Come up with a plan. There's a reason the grand wizard sent me to you."

Travis spun around, trying to come up with something, anything. "Guys, what if we can distract him enough that Woodstock and Quack can get the wand."

"How?" Madison said.

Travis bent down and picked up a small rock. Marcus looked at him, smiled, and grabbed some rocks.

"You're gonna throw rocks at a person?" Madison said.

"We'll keep them low," Travis said.

"That's not a good—" Madison didn't complete her sentence before both Travis and Marcus both hurled rocks at E.W.

"Oh, no," Travis said. "Run."

Neither of the boys actually hit E.W., but they did get his attention. The wizard turned toward them, his wand pointed their way. The kids scattered on their bikes. They regrouped minutes later, out of sight of E.W.

"Hey, where's Madison?" Stacey asked.

"I thought she was with us," Marcus said.

"Baako. Is there any chance you can make us invisible?" Travis asked.

"No. I told you I ..." The eagle stopped mid-sentence. She let out a shrill bird call, the sound of a hawk at the frequency of a hummingbird's chirp. The kids stared at each other. Marcus shrugged. Moments later, Quack and Woodstock flew back, alighting on Marcus's and Stacey's handlebars. Baako glowed, and the two smaller buddies did as well.

"Any other requests for magical powers, for your buddies?" Baako asked.

Madison pulled up on her bike. "Yeah, can you unfreeze Tiger?"

"You went back?" Stacey said.

"Yeah, and I wish you had too." Stacey opened her mouth to say something, but Madison didn't give her a chance. "No, I'm not blaming you. It's just that E.W. started running after you, and he dropped his wand. If one of you had been there, we might have picked it up."

Baako glowed. Tiger stretched and meowed. The light coming from Baako intensified. Three separate yellowish blue bands of light erupted from the eagle and flowed into each of the buddies.

"What'd you do?" Travis asked.

Baako didn't answer but instead uttered a command. "Grab Quack." Marcus grabbed the duck off his handlebars.

"Quack, will you please disappear," Baako said.

"I know I messed up, but do I really have to go?" The duck sounded miserable.

"No, no, dear friend. I merely want you to become invisible."

"Oh." If ever a duck looked confused, that was Quack. Marcus's face wore a similar expression, until he disappeared, along with the duck.

"How's that?" Came Quack's voice.

"Excellent. Now, come back."

Quack and Marcus reappeared in the same spot.

"No way!" Travis said.

"Wow!" Madison said.

Stacey's mouth was slightly agape, and she appeared to have lost her ability to talk.

"The buddies can now perform other magic, should you need them to."

"Can't you help?" Travis implored.

"If I am captured, it could spell the end of merciful magic, and the wizard would become unstoppable."

"Yeah, you should just stay out of it," Marcus said.

"Now is the time to use your brains. Surely you can come up with better ideas than throwing rocks."

Travis and Marcus glanced at each other, abashed. Then Marcus seemed to perk up. "I've got an idea."

Chapter 14

Woodstock took off from Stacey's bike, returning minutes later. "He's walking down the road, heading back toward town."

"He's not even trying to hide?" Stacey asked.

Woodstock shook his feathered head.

"How far down is he?" Madison asked.

"About thirty seconds."

"Huh?"

"Or maybe thirty miles?"

"You have no idea where he is, do you?" Stacey said.

"Do too. He's on the road walking to town."

Woodstock sounded offended.

"Let's just go," Madison said.

"Um." Marcus suddenly looked worried. His eyes widened before he hung his head. He shifted weight from one leg to the other. "Um," he repeated. "Are we sure this is going to work?"

"It's your idea!" Stacey said accusingly.

Travis stepped up to the side of his friend. "It's a good plan, Marcus. And the only one we've got." Travis glared at Stacey, daring her to say something else to his best friend. "Unless you have another idea?"

Stacey shook her head.

"Ok then. Come on." Travis play punched Marcus on the shoulder. "We've got this." Travis sounded more confident than he felt.

Marcus gave Travis the beginnings of a smile and nodded.

"Travis, would you please put me in your backpack," Baako said. "But don't zip it all the way."

"In case you need to come out and help?" Travis asked eagerly.

"No. I'm claustrophobic. And your bag stinks."

"You just like to get right to the point, don't you?" Travis grabbed the eagle and placed her in his backpack, leaving an opening large enough she could get out if needed.

The plan called for Marcus, invisible with the help of Quack, to sneak up behind E.W., crouch down on all fours and have the others surprise him so that he backed up and fell over Marcus.

But it wasn't meant to be.

Travis teamed up with Stacey and Madison, pedaling their bikes through the trees, out of sight from the road, before doubling back to confront the wizard as he headed back to town. But at the same moment E.W. came into view, something rushed past Travis.

"Let's get out of here!" Marcus cried. He was no longer invisible. Standing up on his bike, pedaling ferociously, he clearly wanted to be anywhere else but where he was. The others took off after him, putting distance between themselves and E.W.

Marcus didn't stop until he was back at his house.

"What gives?" Stacey skidded her bike next to Marcus. Travis arrived immediately after and heard her throw the question at Marcus.

Travis jumped off his bike and stood next to his best friend. "I'm sure he has his reasons," Travis said.

"Roger." Marcus gasped, trying to catch his breath. "I went to ditch my bike … so I could sneak up on E.W. … and Roger was right there. I just couldn't …" His voice trailed off. He leaned over his handlebars, breathing hard.

"It's okay," Travis said. "We'll just come up with a different plan."

The front door of Marcus's house opened. "Marcus." His mom stood in the doorway, a blue apron decorated with blotches of flour tied around her waist. "There you are. Did you finish your homework?"

"I don't have any."

His mother's eyebrows disappeared into her forehead.

"Well, maybe a little," Marcus said. "But I promise I can finish it after dinner."

"Well, you need a snack at least. Why don't you and your friends come inside. I just pulled out a batch of chocolate chip cookies."

Travis threw down his bike and was up the stairs in a snap, right behind Marcus. He turned at the doorway. Stacey and Madison hadn't moved.

"Come on," Marcus said.

"Yeah," Travis added. He looked first at Stacey, who seemed unsure and Madison, who looked like she was about to object. "I can think better when I'm eating cookies. And Mrs. Robert's are the best."

Stacey and Madison shared a look. Madison shrugged and the corner of Stacey's mouth turned up. They both dropped their bikes and took the stairs two at a time.

"You won't regret it," Travis said.

The smell of chocolate chip cookies hit Travis as he turned into the front hallway. They had his stomach growling and his mouth in a smile. "Thanks, Mrs. Roberts," he said as he took a warm cookie from the plate she held out to them.

"Marcus, are you going to introduce me to your new friends?"

"This is Stacey and Madison," he said, pointing to each in turn, "and this is my mom."

"How do you do?" his mom said.

"Hi," the girls chorused.

"Well, don't be shy. Grab a cookie before the boys eat them all." She took a second glance at the kids but merely smiled.

Travis wouldn't have been surprised if she made a comment about their stuffed animals, because Tiger was sitting on Madison's shoulder while Woodstock was perched on Stacey's. He had his hand outstretched to grab another cookie when there was a knock on the door. The four kids looked at each other.

"Get that, Marcus," his mom said. Travis took the opportunity to grab another cookie.

Travis heard the door open, followed by muffled conversation.

"Travis, guys, can you come here?"

Travis exchanged looks with the girls and led the way down the hallway to the front door. He couldn't believe his eyes. In the doorway stood Roger with something in his hand.

"What are you—?" Travis stopped when he realized what Roger held. "Is that Stiff?" Emboldened by his older friends and the safety of Marcus's house, Travis almost said something he knew wasn't nice when he felt a presence behind him.

"Who's at the door?" Mrs. Roberts walked up. "Oh, another friend? Well, invite him in, Marcus." To Roger she said, "Come on in. There's enough cookies for everyone."

Travis's eyes widened, and he started to shake his head no, but Mrs. Roberts stood nearby, waiting, as if she knew something was amiss. Marcus backed up, giving Roger room to pass into the house. Stacey and Madison eyed him from the edge of the room.

"Thank you," Roger said in a kind, timid voice Travis wouldn't have thought possible coming from him. Roger stood awkwardly in front of the closed door. The five kids stood in an uncomfortable silence. Mrs. Roberts sized up the group.

"Marcus," she barked. "Where are your manners?"

"Roger," Marcus said, "come on this way."

Roger handed Stiff to Travis as he walked by. Roger didn't even glance at Travis. Odd behavior for someone who never passed up an opportunity to get a jab in at school. Travis was too shocked to move.

From the kitchen came the sound of Marcus's voice. "Mom, can we take this out back?"

"Sure, sweetie. But wrap it up soon. I don't want anyone's mom calling me complaining I ruined you alls dinner." There was a laughter and warmth in her voice that Travis loved.

"Travis, come on." Travis followed the sound of Marcus's voice out of the house and into the backyard. Encircled by an eight-foot tall wooden fence, the yard was the size of a basketball court and sported a hoop at one end.

Marcus stared at Roger, the plate of cookies in his hand. Roger didn't have any cookies, and Travis was secretly glad.

"Why you showing up here?" Marcus's voice held a hint of fear, something Travis only noticed because they were best friends. He doubted anyone else did.

Roger kept his head down and his eyes averted. "Sorry about your … whatever that was. It was dead when I found it."

Travis looked down at his hand. Stiff was on his back, eyes closed, legs in the air. "Where'd you find it?"

"That guy. I don't know his name. He tossed it aside after he zapped it."

Chapter 15

"You here to spy on us?" Travis asked accusingly.

"No." Roger looked up momentarily before dropping his gaze.

"Marcus, let me have those," Madison said, relieving Marcus of the plate of cookies.

"Roger, have a cookie," Madison said, holding the plate out to Roger.

"What?"

"Hey!"

Madison quieted both Travis and Marcus with a look. "Give him a chance, okay?"

Travis scoffed. Marcus crossed his arms on his chest.

"Are you helping whatever his name is?" Marcus said, accusation in his voice.

Roger shook his head.

"We call him E.W.," Madison added. "It's just easier."

Roger looked at her questioningly.

"E.W. Evil Wizard."

Roger nodded his understanding.

"So," Travis nearly spat, "you working with him?"

Roger shook his head again. "No. I mean, I was. At first. But then …" His head went down as he swallowed his words.

"But then, what?" Travis snapped.

"Guys," Stacey said, "can you at least try and be nice?"

"You have no idea what he's put us through," Travis said, exasperated.

"He's mean," Marcus added.

That last comment had an effect on Roger that Travis didn't expect. Having faced his accusers as they spoke, a sadness filled Roger's eyes.

"Guys, stop," Madison said.

"No," Roger said. "They're right. I don't blame them for not wanting me here."

Roger started to head toward the back door, an uneaten cookie in his hand.

Madison insisted, with a silent glare, that Travis and Marcus do something.

"Wait," Travis found himself saying. "What happened? With E.W.?"

Roger stopped but kept his back to them. "I thought it would be fun to play tricks on you. But ends up, he's really, really mean. He tricked," Roger turned around to face Travis, "whatever that is," his eyes found Stiff, "into talking to him, but killed him anyways."

The group stood, silent and awkward. Roger shifted from side to side on his feet.

"So you just left?" Marcus asked.

Roger nodded. "He got really mad after he zapped that thing." Roger's eyes flitted to Stiff, still in Travis's hand.

"What did he say?" Madison asked, curiosity evident in her voice.

Roger shrugged. "Something about it not working."

"What not working?" Madison said. Travis couldn't understand why Madison seemed so interested in what Roger had to say.

"I remember he said …" Roger's eyes rolled skyward. "I need more power. This has nothing." Roger faced Madison. "Yeah, I'm pretty sure that's what he said. Then he took that wand of his and waved it at a tree, like he wanted to cut it down. He was so angry."

"What happened?" Madison said.

"He knocked an old bird's nest down."

"Oh." Madison seemed to deflate.

"What?" Stacey asked. "Did you expect something else to happen?"

"I was hoping he was losing his powers."

"Why would he lose his powers?" Marcus asked.

Roger's eyes lit up as he looked at Marcus.

"What? Why you looking at me like that?"

"He went all crazy after the nest fell down," Roger said. He waved his wand at the tree, yelling, like he was cursing it, and buds and a few leaves fell off, but it only seemed to make him madder."

"So maybe he is losing his powers," Stacey said.

"What if," Madison said, "when he tries to steal power, he actually loses it? Or maybe when he tries to hurt or kill, he loses some?"

"Oh," Stacey said. "Was it only me, or did you all feel like you were being tickled that other day when he broke into your house?" She looked at Travis.

"No, me too," Travis said. "And you," he looked at Marcus, "busted out laughing so hard."

"Same," Madison said.

"And didn't he say that we should have been in pain instead?" Stacey said.

The others nodded.

"I assumed Baako protected us, but maybe she didn't need to."

"Who's Baako?" Roger asked.

"None of your—" Marcus started.

Madison interrupted him. "Are you really here to help?" she asked Roger.

He stared directly into her eyes. "Yes."

"Yeah, right," Travis said.

Marcus shook his head and glanced at the ground.

"Hey," Roger said.

Travis couldn't believe it. Roger's eyes appeared to be glistening. He fought back the urge to laugh at him.

"I'm sorry for being so …" Roger paused, appearing to struggle to say what came next. "... for being so mean." He took a deep breath. "When I saw E.W. kill your ... what is that?"

"An Opossum," Travis said.

"It made me sick to my stomach. I saw how mean he was and ... I don't want to be like him."

Everyone stood still, not saying anything. Roger stared at the ground. Marcus looked up and found Travis. They had a brief, silent conversation. Travis shrugged. Marcus nodded.

"Okay," Marcus said.

"Okay, what?" Stacey said.

"I accept his apology," Marcus said.

"Why are you telling me?" Stacey said.

Marcus sighed and turned to Roger. "I accept your apology."

Roger looked up. The expression of relief on his face shook Travis. A tear rolled down the big kid's cheek.

"What about you, Travis?" Madison asked.

Travis nodded, unable to find his voice.

"We do need all the help we can get," Madison said.

"I know," Marcus whispered.

"Okay," Madison said to Roger. "You can stay if you'll help us." She turned to the others. "Everyone okay with that?"

Everyone nodded.

"Whew," a voice said from Travis's hand. He looked down and Stiff was rolling over from his back, up onto his feet. "Even opossums don't like to play dead forever."

"What?" Travis said, astonished.

The rest of the group broke up laughing except Roger, who stood with his mouth hanging open.

"I thought he zapped you," Roger said.

"Oh, he did. And it didn't feel good. But it didn't kill me either. Nor did he take away my powers. He seems to be getting weaker."

A voice came from behind Travis, who was still wearing his backpack. "Sometimes when one tries to take what is not theirs, they lose what they had." Baako's head poked out of the backpack.

"Do they all talk?" Roger asked.

"Yes, we do." Tiger spoke from his perch on Madison's shoulder.

Roger took a step back, perhaps remembering his first encounter with the cat.

"Baako," Marcus asked, "what did you mean ... what you just said? I don't get it."

"When we steal from others, whether power or possessions, we lose something within ourselves." Travis sensed Baako turn her head. "This dear boy knows of what I am speaking."

Roger nodded. "I thought taking your stuff and pushing you around would make me feel better. But it didn't. I felt worse. It's awful having no friends."

At that moment, a part of Travis almost felt sad for Roger. But a voice inside his head said, "Serves you right."

"Wait. So you're saying that E.W. loses his powers when he tries to hurt our buddies or take their powers?" Marcus asked Baako.

"Exactly."

"Then I have a plan," Marcus said. The others looked at him skeptically. "No, really. This one I can do," he said.

At that moment, Mrs. Roberts opened the back door. "It's time you all got back home. Marcus needs to come in for dinner."

"Okay," Marcus said. "Can I have two more minutes?"

"One." Mrs. Roberts held up her index finger.

Marcus nodded, and she closed the door.

"Meet back here tomorrow morning, ten o'clock. Bring whatever stuffed animals or action figures you have."

"What—?" Stacey started to say, but Marcus interrupted her.

"Just trust me, please. If I try and explain now, my mom will let you all see how mad she can get."

"Okay, okay."

The kids filed back into and through the house. As they left, Marcus called out, "You, too, Roger."

"What are you doing?" hissed Travis. On the top step, he turned to face Marcus.

"He apologized," Marcus said. "And he looked miserable when he said he had no friends."

Travis shook his head, turned, and headed down the stairs.

"Travis," Marcus said.

Travis paused but didn't turn around. "What?" His voice sounded mad, almost mean. He hadn't meant it to come out that way.

"Nothing."

Travis wasn't sure what to do or say so he walked away, leaving his best friend to watch him go.

Chapter 16

That night at dinner, Travis picked at his food. He mind-lessly twirled spaghetti on his fork.

"You gonna eat that, sport?" his dad said.

"Huh?" Travis looked at his dad before dropping his gaze down to his plate. "Oh, yeah." He took a bite.

"What's wrong, son?" His dad put his fork down, giving Travis his full attention.

Out of the corner of his eye, Travis could see his mom still eating, but he knew she was watching and listening.

Travis shrugged. His dad waited.

"It's just ... there's this bully at school."

"Did he steal your lunch money again?" his mom said.

Travis shook his head. "No. He apologized for being mean. He said he had no friends."

"That's great," his mom said.

Travis shrugged again and dipped his head. His parents didn't say anything. The clink of his mom's fork on her plate told him he had her full attention, and that he couldn't avoid talking about this.

"It's just …" Travis looked up, turning from one parent to the other across the table, "he's been so mean for so long."

"You're not sure you can forgive him."

Travis eyed his dad before nodding.

"Forgiveness is hard. But if you hold on to your anger, it will only hurt you." His dad broke eye contact and glanced at his mom.

"This boy," his mom said. "Do you have any idea why he's a bully?"

Travis shook his head at first. But the image of an adult yelling at Roger came back to him, and Travis nodded. "I don't think his parents are very nice to him."

"How would it feel to have parents who weren't nice to you?" His mom's voice sounded soft, barely more than a whisper.

Travis looked up at his mom. "It would be awful."

"Sometimes when we're mad or scared, and we don't know how to talk about it, we can lash out at others. If this boy doesn't have anyone to talk to, he may not know any other way."

"I guess," Travis said, twirling spaghetti onto his fork again and taking a bite. He didn't want to talk about Roger anymore. He didn't want to forgive him.

"Just try to put yourself in his shoes," his dad said.

***

Ten o'clock the next morning found Travis at Marcus's house along with Stacey and Madison, but no Roger. Though he kept it to himself, Travis was glad. He didn't want Roger around. He didn't deserve to have any friends. With that thought, a heaviness built up in Travis's chest. What if Roger had heard Travis complain to Marcus? Maybe it was his fault Roger chose not to come. Or could Roger still be working with E.W?

"Guys, what if—?"

"Can you stop calling us guys?" Stacey said.

"What?" Travis said.

"We're not guys," Madison said.

"Oh, sorry," Travis said.

"It's okay," Stacey said. "You were saying?"

"What if Roger was pretending yesterday? What if he's still working with E.W.?"

"Then what's he doing here with his action figures?" Madison said.

Travis turned with the others to watch Roger approach on his bike. He seemed hesitant, almost shy. In one hand he held a miniature Spider-Man. His other hand gripped the handlebar and the leg of a much larger Batman.

"Hi," Madison and Stacey chorused.

"Hey," Marcus said.

Travis barely managed a nod. He couldn't help realizing that he and Roger brought the same action figures, though Roger's Batman was much larger than his own.

"Okay," Madison said. "What's your plan?"

"E.W. assumes he can take power from our buddies, but he can't. It makes him weaker, right?"

The others nodded.

"So what if Baako gives our action figures magic? Then E.W. tries to steal their powers. If we have enough of them, maybe it will be enough to take the wizard's powers away."

Everyone stood staring at Marcus.

"Well," he said, putting his head down, "I thought it was a good plan."

Madison found her voice first. "Marcus, it's brilliant."

Marcus looked up. "Really?"

"Yes. Really," Travis said.

Stacey smiled and nodded approvingly.

Roger didn't respond, still holding his head down.

Travis pulled his backpack off his shoulder. Inside, he'd stuffed his Spider-man and Batman action figures as well as Stiff. Baako's head stuck out the top. "Can you do it, Baako?"

The eagle nodded.

"Any idea where we should try this?" Stacey asked.

"By the river," Roger said, having finally stopped staring at the ground.

"Why there?" Travis asked, unable to hold back the contempt in his voice. "He almost caught us at the river yesterday."

"Because I told him that was where you hang out on Saturday mornings."

"Why would you do that?" Travis said.

"When I was walking home yesterday, he was waiting for me. I told him I'd pretended to apologize and that you invited me to hang out with you at the river. I figured whatever plan you had," he looked at Marcus, "would work there."

Travis looked at him, speechless.

"He believed you?" Marcus asked.

Roger shrugged. "I think so."

"Okay, let's—" Madison started.

"Wait," Travis interrupted. "How do we know you're not lying to us? Maybe he's waiting at the river for us and this is a trap."

"I'm not. I swear," Roger said.

"Prove it," Travis said. The words of his parents came back to him, but he pushed them away. Roger didn't deserve his forgiveness. But then he looked at Roger, really looked at him. He looked crestfallen; his eyes glistened. The words of Travis' parents came back to him. "How do you think it would feel …?"

Roger dipped his head. Travis sensed the others watching. "Never mind," he said. "You're here, with us." He knew it wasn't enough, but it was all he could manage for the moment.

"What time did you tell him we'd be at the river?" Madison asked.

"Eleven."

"Then we need to get going," Madison said.

Twenty minutes later, their bikes were stashed in the trees along the riverside. Another fifteen minutes, and they were set up and ready.

"What time is it?" Stacey asked.

"Ten-fifty," Madison said.

"Ten minutes to spare," Marcus said.

If the wizard is actually coming. Travis kept the thought to himself.

Chapter 17

Eleven o'clock came, but there was no sign of E.W. As the minutes ticked by, the kids looked from one to another, shrugging or shaking their heads. Eleven-ten came and went. Stacey and Madison sat down on the boulders lining the river. Travis paced amongst the trees, his feet crunching fallen twigs underfoot. Marcus stood leaning against a tree. Roger stood off to the side, his head down. At eleven-fifteen, Travis could take it no longer. He rounded on Roger.

"You lied to us, didn't you?" Travis stood directly in front of Roger. He'd forgotten his fear of the bully. For a moment he'd tried to forgive him, but clearly Roger was still up to his old ways.

Roger looked up from the ground but still down to meet Travis's gaze. "I didn't. I swear."

"You're still working with him, aren't you? Just admit it."

Roger shook his head.

Marcus stood at Travis's side. The girls got up and walked toward the boys.

"Why can't you give him a chance?" Madison asked Travis.

"Because he's working with the wizard!" Travis almost shouted the words.

Roger's eyes got big.

"Yes, he is," came a voice behind the group. Everyone turned around, except Roger, who was already facing E.W.

The group froze. The courage Travis felt confronting Roger melted away and was replaced by fear. But not all of it.

"Baako, now!" he managed to yell.

From amongst the trees emerged action figures and stuffed animals of all sizes: miniature Spider-Mans and larger Batmans, a stuffed Tigger and Winnie-the-Pooh. Two brown teddy bears stepped out next to a Barbie doll dressed as a flight attendant with Ken at her side dressed in a baby-blue suit and carrying a suitcase.

"Sorry, guys," Roger said, moving to stand next to the wizard.

"I knew it!" Travis said.

Roger whispered something in the wizard's ear. The man smiled, pulled out his wand, and stepped forward. "Now, the power will be mine!" His words sounded as if they came from a triumphant, crazy person, punctuated as they were with maniacal laughter.

Travis started forward, but Madison grabbed his arm. She pulled him back until he turned on his own accord and ran with the others behind a boulder.

"Why'd you pull me away?" Travis asked angrily.

"Don't you realize?" Madison said.

"Realize what?"

"The wizard is doing exactly what we want him to do. Look."

E.W. pointed his wand at Travis's Spider-Man, who, like the other figures, appeared alive, advancing toward the wizard. The figures, placed in a semi-circle, appeared as if they wanted to surround the wizard, overpower him, perhaps. A miniature army of come-to-life action figures and stuffed animals, a carnival in the woods. The real magical creatures, the buddies born from Baako, were with the detectives.

A blast from the wand knocked over the two-inch action figure. Without hesitation, E.W. turned, pointed his wand at Stacey's teddy bear, muttered an intelligible spell and the bear flew back ten feet, hitting a tree. Barbie was next. She soared through the air and landed on a rock. "Too bad she didn't explode," Madison said. "I never liked that doll." As the wizard turned, she added, "Oh, I hope Ken gets blasted in two."

Travis turned his head, knowing his face must have worn a befuddled expression.

"You ever get a girly doll you never wanted?"

Travis shook his head.

"Then you wouldn't understand." Madison pointed.

Travis returned his attention to the wizard, who wore a smile reminiscent of a deranged lunatic. He threw his head back in laughter before pointing his wand, first at Travis's Batman and then Roger's. As the action figures flew backwards into the forest, as E.W. turned to what he might have supposed was his last victim, Roger's Spider-Man, his back was to his original targets. Targets which were now back on their feet and advancing. Confusion replaced triumph on his face as he witnessed a miniature Spider-Man and a teddy bear approaching.

"What?" His voice held both confusion and rage.

He pointed his wand and blasted each figure in turn, faster this time, the smile wiped from his face.

From behind Travis's back, an eagle cry sounded. The wizard paid it no heed. Understandable, for Baako's cry was close to that of a true eagle. Also, the wizard seemed to become crazier with each blast of his wand.

"He's getting weaker, look," Madison said. Travis realized it right before she spoke. The blasts from E.W.'s wand were not only dimmer, but the enchanted action figures were being pushed back, but not knocked over. Which is perhaps why Baako sounded her call to action when she did.

Following the eagle's cry, the truly magical creatures—Stiff, Tiger, Quack and Woodstock—left the sidelines and approached the wizard in a coordinated attack. With the wizard's back turned, the birds approached by air, while Tiger and Stiff covered the short distance on the ground. Travis hadn't known an opossum could move so quickly.

Stiff appeared to bite the wizard on the leg while at the same time, Tiger launched herself into the air, digging her claws into his butt. The plan was for her to aim for his back, but clearly, she didn't jump high enough. Though perhaps it was better this way. It definitely got his attention. He swiped behind him with his wand hand, probably on instinct as it surely was his dominant hand, and at that moment, Woodstock sunk his talons into his wrist while Quack grabbed the wand with her beak. The owl's talons had the desired effect as E.W. relaxed his grip on the wand just enough for the duck to grab it from his hand.

The magic buddies returned to Travis, Marcus, Stacey and Madison, now standing as a group and no longer hiding. Out of the corner of his eye, Travis saw Madison gesture to Roger, standing off to the side by himself, where he'd been forgotten in the mayhem of the moment. To Travis's amazement, Roger came and stood at Madison's side.

"Nice work," she said.

"Thanks," Roger said, glancing over at Travis as he spoke.

"You … you really were helping us?" Travis stammered.

Roger nodded.

Before Travis could say anything else, the wizard, clearly furious, and standing in the middle of the small forest clearing, caught his attention. "Silly children. I don't need my wand to do magic. It merely makes it easier to focus my powers." He raised both arms, so they stretched out toward the group. "Admar prochinum!" he shouted.

Travis didn't know what the spell was supposed to do, but it seemed to cause a soft breeze to brush against his skin. As he and the others stood, unaffected by the spell, E.W. worked himself up into a tizzy. "Admar prochinum!" he shouted again. "Admar prochinum!"

"It's over," Madison said, stepping forward. "You cannot steal magic that is not yours."

It wasn't clear if the wizard heard beyond Madison's first words. "It's not over!" he screamed.

"Travis," Baako said from his hideout in the backpack strapped to Travis's back. "It's your turn."

Chapter 18

Travis took off the backpack, reached in and pulled out a toy helicopter. Parting with it was difficult, as it was his favorite toy. Battery operated, its rotors spun; one push button made the sound of rotating blades while another sounded a siren. But what they needed now was the wench with a hook at the end that could be lowered from the base. Travis grabbed his miniature Spider-Man. Roger handed Travis his own Spider-Man action figure, the two boys exchanging a glance as the toy switched hands. Without meaning to, Travis gave him a small smile. Roger smiled back.

Travis placed the two toys into the helicopter. Baako glowed once more from within her hideout, and the helicopter and action figures responded. The helicopter lifted silently into the air. Roger's action figure sat in the cockpit while Travis's stood in the door.

E.W. continued to shout spells, having switched to a different incantation that caused the faintest tickling sensation in Travis's feet. Distracted as he was, the wizard didn't notice the helicopter rise into the air and fly over his head.

As the winch descended behind the wizard, Travis realized they needed to keep him distracted. "Hey," he shouted, stepping forward. "What's wrong? Lost your powers or something?"

E.W. turned toward Travis, the look of hatred on the wizard's face making Travis take a step back. The wizard, while having lost most of his powers, was still a full-grown man and Travis, average height for his age, was still a child of ten. Travis gulped. E.W. took a step toward Travis. But at that moment, the winch, lowered by Travis's own action figure, hooked onto the belt loop of the wizard's pants. Woodstock, having flown unnoticed to the base of the helicopter's tow line, placed the hook through his belt loop. The wizard's second step missed the ground as the helicopter rose into the air. From the looks of it, when the helicopter picked the wizard up off the ground, it gave him a wedgie. His face contorted in pain and his hands reached for his behind.

"What? What? Get me down! Right now! What are you doing? Where are you taking me? I demand—"

But what he demanded they never heard. For the chopper, reaching a height above the trees, turned and flew away, making the wizard's words unintelligible.

The group on the ground stood and followed the helicopter as it flew out of sight.

"Where do you think he'll end up?" asked Marcus, his head still facing the sky.

"Hopefully far enough away," Stacey said, "that he'll think twice about coming back."

"He'll be back." Roger stood apart from the group, shoulders hunched. His head bowed, he half-heartedly kicked a rock at his feet.

"Why do you say that?" Madison asked. She took a step toward him.

"Because he told me." Roger looked up at Madison, seemingly avoiding the others. "He said that he'd do whatever it took to get more power. Whatever it took. Those were his exact words."

"Then we'll just have to be ready," Madison said with a steely resolve. She walked over and picked the discarded wand off the ground.

"What are you going to do with that?" Travis asked.

Madison stared at it for a second before opening Travis's backpack and shoving it inside. "Let's deal with that later."

Roger's head was bowed again. It reminded Travis of being left out of a dodgeball game back in the third grade.

"Hey." Travis looked at Roger, whose head remained downcast. Travis tried again. "Hey, Roger." His voice was soft, quiet. The others stood, waiting silently. Roger glanced at Travis.

"Thanks for your help. And sorry I didn't trust you sooner. It's just … the toilet? Why'd you have to do that? And always taking my money. It's not cool. It's just not." Travis looked away, mad and ashamed he'd said so much. The worst thing to do was to let a bully know he got to you.

"I'm sorry." The crack in Roger's voice made Travis turn back to face him. "I really am." A tear formed in the corner of Roger's eye. "You, too," Roger said, directing his statement at Marcus.

Marcus caught Travis's attention. They had a silent conversation only best friends can have. Marcus shrugged, suggesting to Travis that they forgive Roger. Travis eyed Marcus, questioning his judgment. Marcus met Travis's gaze, insisting it was for the best. When the two finally turned away from each other, it was to find the others staring at them.

"What was that?" Stacey said, wagging her finger from one boy to the other.

"That was them trying to figure out if they could forgive me," Roger said.

"How'd you know that?" Travis said.

"I've been watching you since kindergarten. You have these silent conversations a lot."

"We do?" Marcus said.

The girls laughed.

Roger shifted uncomfortably from one foot to the other. "I always wanted friends like you. I even asked to play with you once, but you said no."

"What?" Travis said, shocked. "When?"

"In kindergarten." Roger's face flushed. "I ... it doesn't matter."

Travis stared at Roger, wracking his brain for a memory but coming up empty. He turned to Marcus, but he merely shrugged.

"So, can you all call a truce?" Madison asked.

The three boys looked at one another and nodded.

"Shake on it," Stacey said.

"What?" Travis said. He started to say, "No," but bit his tongue.

Marcus stepped forward and put out his hand. Roger reached out and took Marcus's and they shook. They let go. Roger stood waiting. In that moment, shoulders hunched, shame crowding his face, he no longer seemed the bully Travis feared. He seemed more like a kid who needed a friend. Travis stepped up and offered his hand. Roger looked up at him, his eyes betraying his craving for acceptance and forgiveness.

"Next time," Travis said as they shook, "maybe ask again to join in a game. 'Cause I really don't remember."

The corner of Roger's mouth turned up in the smallest hint of a smile. "Yeah. Okay."

"Boys," Stacey said, directing her comment to Madison. The two exchanged a smile.

"What?" Marcus and Travis said.

"Nothing," the girls chorused.

"Finally," Baako said. "Let me out, please." Travis pulled the bag off his shoulder, undid the zipper all the way, and Baako stepped out. She immediately ruffled her feathers, spread her wings and took to the sky.

"Baako?" Travis called out.

"Where's she off to?" Stacey asked.

"No idea," Travis said.

"As far away from your backpack as possible," Marcus said, picking up the bag, sniffing it and making a face. "Yep, that's probably it."

"Very funny," Travis said. "It doesn't smell that—" He put the bag up to his nose. "Oh man, it stinks. Wow! I had no idea."

Everyone broke out laughing, including Roger.

"Yeah, yeah, very funny." Travis said it like he was perturbed but smiled at the same time. "First one to my house wins." He jumped on his bike. "You too, Roger." Roger didn't hesitate before jumping on his bike, joining the others as they rode down the dirt road.

ABOUT THE AUTHOR

While she works as a physical therapist, Sussi Voak rises before the sun to follow her writing dreams. This is her fourth book in the TDC series. Raised in the Santa Cruz Mountains of California, Sussi Voak currently lives in Philadelphia with her son.Visit her author page at sussivoak.com, and please consider writing a review on Amazon or Goodreads to help spread the word about this book.